TRAFALGAR VERSUS BOONE

Book Seven of Trafalgar and Boone

Geonn Cannon

Supposed Crimes LLC • Matthews, North Carolina

This book is a work of fiction. Names, characters, places, and incidents are products of the author's imagination or are used fictitiously. Any resemblance to actual events or locales or persons, living or dead, is entirely coincidental.

Published in the United States.

ISBN: 978-1-952150-21-0

www.supposedcrimes.com

This book is typeset in Goudy Old Style.

When we last visited our intrepid heroes...

The partnership between DOROTHY BOONE and MISS TRAFALGAR had come to an ignominious end. A protective curse on an ancient queen's gravesite felled not only Trafalgar but infected all of London with a fatal virus, forcing Dorothy to take extreme measures to prevent a catastrophe. Her actions stopped the illness, but the people of London were imbued with new and dangerous magical abilities.

To put things right, BEATRICE SEK and the other three elementals united at the Tower of London to create the fifth elemental: void. Their plan worked, and magic was effectively dampened, but at a tremendous cost. Beatrice has apparently lost her life, and Dorothy's rash actions during the crisis led to a rift with Trafalgar which eventually led to an agreement to part ways.

The world marches on. The MNEMOSYNE SOCIETY continues to grow and thrive, with the former members of the Forty Elephants proving themselves worthy new additions to the ranks. Scotland Yard has come to respect the contributions of the group and often consults them in situations that have a supernatural bent.

It has been seven years since Dorothy Boone and Miss Trafalgar were alone in a room together, but that is soon to change.

PROLOGUE

1930
Valencia, Spain

TRAFALGAR RHYS had never seen an orange more ripe for the plucking. It hung on the end of a long branch which extended out over the stone wall so that she didn't even have to leave the road to grab it. She pulled gently and it came free with barely any pressure. It was heavy in her hand, the rind dotted with water droplets. She looked over the wall at the perfectly-lined rows of identical trees stretching out toward the horizon. The unbelievable green of the trees and the brilliantly blue sky made the fruit look golden.

"I don't believe I've ever seen so much orange in my entire life."

"Then perhaps you can spare one for a hungry traveler."

Trafalgar smiled and tossed the orange to her right without bothering to aim.

Violet Rhys let go of her reins with one hand to catch it. She brought it to her mouth, broke the skin with her teeth, and proceeded to peel it with one hand.

"Deft fingers," Trafalgar noted.

"Not so bad with my mouth, either," Violet said with a wink.

Trafalgar smiled.

Their horses, rented from a man in Valencia, plodded along side-by-side in the center of the road. The outskirts of town were still a hazy outline on the horizon behind them. Ahead, they could see the scattered stone structures of vineyards and the buildings that served the grove Trafalgar had just stolen from. They were dressed casually in riding pants, knee-high leather boots, and button-down shirts under light jackets. Trafalgar wore sunglasses, and Violet had covered her blonde curls with a maroon boater.

When they reached an intersection, Trafalgar looked to Violet for guidance. Violet gestured to the left with her chin and Trafalgar nudged her horse in that direction. She immediately saw their probable destination and turned back for confirmation. Violet nodded again, shrugged, and her eyebrows rose.

"That's where they are."

"Interesting." Trafalgar faced forward again.

The road dead-ended at a tall stone building a hundred yards ahead. The façade was cracked and broken to reveal the brickwork underneath. The windows had all been covered by planks of wood which were painted with colorful circus scenes of animals, acrobats, and aerialists. A wooden archway over the entrance declared it was the site of the Valbuena Traveling Circus. The field to the east of the building was filled with trailers she assumed housed the talent, while the field on the opposite side of the building housed a trio of tents of various sizes.

Trafalgar halted her horse a fair distance away and took off her sunglasses. Violet came to a stop beside her. They had been hired to find twin girls who had gained magical abilities during what had come to be known as the Awakening of 1923. The vast majority of Londoners who were affected by the magical storm lost their power when Beatrice Sek and the other elementals created "void," but it hadn't returned everyone to normal. Some retained their unique talents, and no one had been able to determine exactly why some people were unaffected by the void. Trafalgar knew several members of the Mnemosyne Society were hard at work investigating it but they were no closer to a solution now than they'd been seven years ago.

Violet was one of the lucky few who still had her power. She was blessed with the ability to find anything, no matter where it was in the world. It worked with people as well as objects, and they'd built a strong reputation for being able to find the unfindable for both citizens and the constables of London who found themselves stumped in a case.

In all the time they'd worked together, Trafalgar had never

known Violet to be wrong, so she didn't bother questioning her guidance. She searched for the area for signs of life. A stone wall obscured the area around the tents, but she could hear voices and the sound of construction work occurring just out of sight.

"Options," Trafalgar said. "We walk in now under the guise of roustabouts in search of work, and use the job as an opportunity to dig around. Or we can go get some rest, come back tonight as paying customers, and snoop around then."

"The best part about working as a team is that we don't have to choose between two good ideas."

Trafalgar held out her fist. "Odds. Loser does the grunt work, winner plays the rube."

Violet held her fist next to Trafalgar's. "Once, twice, thrice, shoot."

They went best of three, and Violet ended up the winner. Trafalgar could tell she was trying to hide her smugness as she took up her reins again.

"You've said several times your ability can't determine future positions of objects, correct?"

Violet nodded. "It's location, not premonition. Why?"

"You win at roshambo far too much. I'm beginning to suspect you know what my hand is going to do."

"Ah." Violet's lips twisted into a smile. "Perhaps I am just a connoisseur of your hand's capabilities."

"Flirt." She winked and smiled, brushing her fingers suggestively across her lips.

Violet sighed. "It worked out well in the end, wouldn't you say? I make a far more convincing genteel lady, and you're much better at the grunt work."

"Are you calling me the muscle?"

Violet tossed her head so that her curls bounced. "Are you denying that I'm the beauty...?"

Trafalgar pursed her lips to keep from smiling. "Very well. I'll abide by the rules of the game. You go back to the boardinghouse and get some rest. At least one of us will be rested if this goes into the evening. I'll do my best to get hired and see what I can discover from the workers."

"Okay." Violet leaned across the distance between them, and Trafalgar met her in the middle for a kiss. Trafalgar tasted the remnants of the orange's juices on her lips. "Be safe, wife."

Trafalgar smiled. "I'll see you soon, wife."

Violet clucked her tongue to turn her horse around, and Trafalgar twisted to watch her ride away. She only watched until Violet turned around, and they waved once more at each other. Her wife. Her beloved. She'd never seen herself in a marriage until she realized that men weren't her only option. She was attracted to them, could muster up enough feelings to sleep with one, but love? She apparently only reserved that for women. Her first two female lovers had made matrimony seem plausible. Violet, her truest love, had made it essential.

Trafalgar faced forward again and focused on the building, pushing away the distracting thoughts of the woman who had finally given her a last name. She took a deep breath and dismounted her horse, leading it the rest of the way down the road to the double-wide front doors of the Valbuena Traveling Circus.

She assumed knocking would only get her someone in management, so she hitched her horse to the available post and walked along the wall until she found a gate. It was unlocked so she let herself in and found herself in a tent city. Rows of identical tents filled the space, flanked on both ends by walls of wheeled trailers that had barred windows high on their sides. She smelled the unmistakable stench of animals, the waste and food and hay, that was almost covered by the more inviting scent of freshly-cut wood.

A barrel-chested shirtless man passed by her without a second look. Trafalgar fell into step behind him, hurrying to keep up.

"Is there anywhere I can be of assistance?" she asked him.

"Help from a woman? Do you even know what kind of prep~" He turned and looked at her, slowing slightly as he ran his eyes up and down her body. It felt like a true appraisal of worth rather than anything lascivious, so she allowed it without comment. His jaw clenched, he bobbed his head once, and turned his back on her to keep walking.

"Go down this way," he said, gesturing down one of the lanes between tents. "Find the lady with all the fabrics hung up outside her lot. She's always got more work than hands."

"Much obliged," she said, but he had already moved out of sight behind a trailer.

She took one more look around. A few other circus workers were milling around but, like the strongman, none of them seemed interested in the stranger who had just arrived in their midst.

Secure in their indifference, Trafalgar adjusted her collar and went in search of the woman with the fabrics.

Violet had tried to explain her abilities to many people over the years, but she could never quite articulate exactly how it felt to "sight" things. She didn't see a roadmap projected in front of her eyes, and there was no red line directing her toward whatever hidden treasure someone happened to be seeking. Someone asked her for the location of something. It could be a person, an article of clothing, a book, anything. Once she had an item in mind, she just knew where it was. She could see its surroundings and had a general idea how far away it was in relation to her.

"Think of it this way," she'd once said to Trafalgar while they were lying in bed. "Where are your leather boots?"

"They're~"

Violet had held up a finger. "What are you picturing in your mind?"

"The front closet."

"And while you're not envisioning the entire trip out of the bedroom, down the hall, across the parlor, and into the closet, you're aware of it. You could guide someone there if need be."

Trafalgar had pondered that. "And you can do that with anything?"

Violet shrugged. "So far. Everything I've sought, I ended up finding." She had traced the seam of Trafalgar's night shirt. "I even found some things I wasn't seeking."

Now, as she woke in the boardinghouse they'd been using as a base of operations, Violet spared a thought for Trafalgar and knew she was a mile to the northeast, she was outside, and she was safe. She got out of bed and changed out of her normal attire into something she felt was more in keeping with the rest of the crowd. They'd packed so they could blend in, and she had a pair of dungarees and a threadbare blouse with patches on the sleeves.

It was almost dark when she set out, this time she used the car in case they had a pair of teenaged passengers with them when they left the circus.

Traffic on the road was much heavier now. She joined a line of cars, wagons, and horses which all seemed to share her destination, and she was grateful she could use them as cover. She found a place to leave the car and walked the rest of the way to the building she'd guided them to earlier. The doors were flung open now, and every doorway and window shone with bright golden light. She could also hear music, though at the moment she could only hear a steady drum beat over the sound of chatter from the other patrons on their way inside.

She paid for her ticket at the door and followed the crowd through the building and into the field of tents. Lanterns glowed within every tent and cast odd, inhuman shadows on the canvas walls. Smoke rose from a multitude of cook surfaces, carrying with it the scent of a dozen different foods. Circus workers shouted their offerings, guests exclaimed in wonder and excitement. The cacophony was enough to give Violet a headache, but she powered through. Wooden signs hammered into the ground pointed in various directions, but she didn't need them. She thought of Trafalgar and turned without hesitation to the right.

Her intuition led her to the largest tent. A man took her ticket and directed her to the risers which ringed the perimeter of an open performance area. She took her seat and looked toward the opposite side of the tent where her wife was currently wrapping a rope around a metal peg. She'd also changed clothes; she was now wearing a shirt that bared her muscular arms, and her bald head was covered by a flat cap.

She finished her work and looked up, eyes landing on Violet as if she'd called out. A smile quirked Trafalgar's lips and she touched the brim of her cap. Violet winked. Trafalgar followed another worker behind the rafters and they both ducked through a flap into the darkness beyond.

Violet settled in. The sisters they'd been hired to find were definitely nearby - about a hundred and fifty yards to her right, to be exact - and they were safe. Trafalgar was nearby, so it seemed likely they'd made contact. The girls were named Frieda and Isabel Ickes, and they'd been given the ability to balance on anything. It wasn't very flashy, as magical gifts went, but it certainly made them very good at gymnastics. She could think of a dozen possibilities for circus acts that would be astounding with their skills. Their mission was to discover if the girls had left willingly or if they'd been coerced somehow. If they had been taken, Trafalgar had been tasked with getting them out and bringing them home.

A fanfare of trumpets silenced the crowd. Violet sat up straighter and watched as a man in a flowing red robe and a tall top hat stepped into the center ring with both arms stretched out to either side.

"Ladies and gentlemen!" he bellowed, then repeated it in Spanish as he turned in a slow circle to address the whole crowd. "Welcome to the Valbuena Traveling Circus! Whether this is your first visit with us or a return trip, you are all part of the Valbuena family! And without further ado..." He flicked his wrist and a long walking stick appeared in his hand. He twisted it with his fingers and banged the end on the ground. "*Let the show commence!*"

An unseen band, likely the source of the earlier fanfare, began playing a spritely tune as the performers swept into the ring. Two lions were led out by their trainers, woman in skimpy outfits rode matching horses. A man entered the tent at a full sprint, bounced off a trampoline, and grabbed a ring that hung from a rope. His momentum carried him in a wide arc over the audience, and he smiled and waved as if it was the most ordinary way of entering a room.

Violet had to admit she was impressed by the flood of talent. A man with the beard of a Viking breathed fire. A man in a fancy suit tore off his blazer and shirt to reveal inked designs etched all over his chest and covering his arms. Women somersaulted and juggled. Animals pranced and performed well-choreographed routines for trainers in technicolor suits. The crowd gasped and pointed and struggled to figure out which act was the most deserving of their attention.

Once the show was fully underway and the crowd was entranced by the spectacle, Violet rose and slipped away from the risers and out of the tent. She only had to pause for a second to know which way to go, and she went there quickly. Even without her ability, she could have just followed the voices. A man behind the building was on the verge of yelling. As she got closer, she could make out the words.

"~for your incompetence, she could've done a thousand more!"

Trafalgar's voice responded, sounding meek and terrified. "I'm sorry, sir, I don't know what happened. I just wasn't paying attention... I can take her to a medic. There's one in town. Oh, I hope you're not hurt too badly, dear."

A girl started to reply, but the man cut her off. "You're not going anywhere. This girl's got a show to do!"

"Her ankle could be broken!" Trafalgar said. "You can't possibly ask her to perform on that. Maybe her sister~"

"Her sister is already nice and snug. 'Sides, these girls say they can balance on anything. Figure that means broken bones, too. Ain't that right, sweetheart?"

The girl said, "I don't think that's--"

"I said shush!"

Violet took that as her cue and came around the corner. "Did somebody mention a medic?"

Trafalgar was standing next to a man with the face of a mule and the build to match. His legs seemed much too muscular for his body, and his trousers were pulled up high enough to make his torso look truncated. His forearms were wider than his biceps, a peculiarity that she feared meant that he could put a lot of power into a punch... or into crushing things. A girl who matched the photographs they'd been given was lying on the ground between them. All three turned to face Violet.

"Who the blazes are you?" the man said.

"I told you, I'm the medic." She folded her arms behind her and bounced on the balls of her feet, trying to look as much like a schoolmarm as possible. "Would you be a dear and ask me where your weak spot is?"

He narrowed his eyes. "Wot?"

"Say the words 'where is my weak spot'."

"'Where's my weak spot'?" He wrinkled his nose and stalked toward her, squaring up for a punch. "I don't much like punchin' ladies but you got three seconds to--"

"Right ankle," Violet said.

Trafalgar's foot shot out and stomped on the man's foot. It bent in a horrible way, the sound of a snapped bone echoing much louder than it should have. The man's shout was louder, however, and was bound to draw attention. Trafalgar shuffled closer and cracked her elbow across the man's jaw. The errant Ickes sister sprang up like she'd been fired from a catapult and landed hard on the man's back, sending him face-first into the mud.

Violet raised her eyebrows and came closer. "Is this Frieda or Isabel?"

Trafalgar exhaled sharply and rolled her shoulder, checking to make sure she hadn't hurt herself in taking down the brute. "Frieda. Frieda, this is the woman I told you about. The one who is going to help us free your sister."

"She's at the far end of the property, being kept in a shack."

"We know that," Trafalgar said. "We need the key."

Violet said, "Oh." She dropped down and reached into the now-unconscious roustabout's pocket. She pulled out a keyring and held it out to Trafalgar. "There you are."

"My brilliant wife," Trafalgar said, leaning in to kiss Violet as she took the keys.

Frieda observed the kiss with a quickly concealed look of surprise, but she said nothing about it.

"We have to hurry," Trafalgar said, already moving. "We have to assume someone heard him shouting."

Violet and Frieda followed her, the three of them jogging through the maze of trailers.

"Valbuena alternates us," Frieda said to Violet as they ran. "One of us performs while he holds the other prisoner as leverage. We play along, nothing happens to the one of us he's holding."

"That's despicable," Violet said. "Everything will be all right soon. Trafalgar is very--"

A cannonball of a man appeared from nowhere and slammed into Trafalgar from the side. They tangled and hit the ground. Violet moved to help, but another man appeared from behind them and grabbed her arm. Frieda was grabbed by a third man. Violet tugged and tried to slip free, but the grip on her upper arm only tightened.

"She's very good at getting out of tight spaces," Violet muttered, as the cannonball lifted Trafalgar up out of the mud. "That's what I was about to say."

Trafalgar made sure to watch the carny pushing Violet along, keeping track of everything he did that could be construed as damage so she could take it out on him ten-fold. Getting hired had been easy enough; there was always extra work for willing hands on a show day, but every single person she worked with had regarded her as an interloper. No one wanted to talk with her beyond basic directions - "Move that" or "carry this" and whispers fell silent as soon as she came within earshot. She'd quickly found the Ickes sisters and revealed who had sent her, and they revealed their situation.

"We just wanted a bit of excitement," Frieda said. "We had this ability..."

"But there's not a lot of use for balancing skills in day-to-day life," Isabel continued.

"Then the circus came to town."

"We thought it would be a laugh."

"We offered to perform while they were in London."

"It was something to do, and it was great fun."

"But when we went to be paid, Valbuena locked us up."

There were other performers being held against their will, but Trafalgar couldn't promise to save them without knowing what Valbuena's leverage was. She'd intended to sneak Frieda out under the guise of a medical emergency, then go back and get Isabel, and everything had been going perfectly until the last little hiccup.

Granted, it was a pretty sizeable hiccup.

They were taken to the building where Isabel was being held captive. The goon shoved Trafalgar over the threshold, causing her to stumble. The door was closed and locked again by the time she'd regained her balance. She brushed her hands down her arms as if wiping away the man's grip as she turned to examine the others. Violet looked highly annoyed, while the sisters clung to each other with looks of terror.

"Three guards," Violet said without prompting. "Two at the front and another watching the back."

Trafalgar looked around the space for anything they might use to escape. Unsurprisingly, there wasn't a lot to work with. Valbuena was a horrible man, but even he was smart enough not to lock hostages in a room with the means to escape. There was one piece of lumber that could serve as a baseball bat. She picked it up, swung it in a gentle arc to test its weight. Sturdy, but not a lot of help against a locked door. She held onto it, nonetheless.

"In a way we're fortunate," she said. "It's doubtful they'll stop the show, so we have a little time before anyone comes looking for us." She thought for a second and faced Violet, snapping her fingers as if something had just occurred to her. "Darling, where is that thing...?"

Violet frowned. "What thing?"

"The thing we need to secure our escape. You know, the one item we can use to break open this door and dispatch the guards so we can make a clean getaway."

Violet's beautiful blue eyes blinked once at her, and then she wrinkled her brow. "Sorry, my love, but it doesn't work that way. I need a bit more specificity."

"Drat. Worth a try, anyway. I'm open to anyone else's ideas."

Frieda, differentiated by the fact she was the one in costume, looked at Violet. "Can you summon objects to you?"

"Afraid not. I can only point someone to where it is."

Trafalgar had been pacing, but her mind caught on something. "You may not be able to find what we need. But you can find what someone else *wants*."

Violet raised an eyebrow. Trafalgar motioned her toward the door and she followed. "Isabel, Frieda, can the guards hear us through this door?"

"And we can hear them," Isabel said with a sneer of disgust.

Trafalgar knocked on the door. "Gentlemen. We have a proposition for you."

"Boss said you don't get to talk," one of the guards said. "So button your yaps."

"Even if we can give you your heart's desire? Even if we can tell you where to find the one thing you want more than anything else in the world?"

Silence from the other side of the door. Trafalgar waited. Finally, one of the men laughed.

"All right," he chortled. "A Cabriolet. You get me a Cabriolet, I'll open the door for you."

Trafalgar leaned close to Violet. "Where is the key to the nearest Cadillac Cabriolet?"

Violet smiled and raised her voice to be heard through the door. "There's one parked outside the property. The owner left the key underneath the backseat bench."

"Best hurry up, 'fore the show ends and the audience lets out."

More silence. Trafalgar hoped they weren't going to check on the information before following through on the deal. After thirty seconds, she was about to speak again when she suddenly heard the lock click and the door swung open. There was only one man there, and Trafalgar could see the other's back as he hurried his way down the aisle between trailers.

The remaining guard put his hand on the door frame, blocking their exit. He smiled as he examined the four women inside.

"He wanted a car... what about what *I* want?"

"Well, sure, that's only fair." Violet's voice was sweetness and light, lilting and gentle. "But there's one little problem, dear."

"And what's that, buttercup?"

Violet shrugged and looked disappointed in him. "You've already opened the door."

He didn't have time to consider her meaning before Trafalgar smacked her lumber bat into his face. The man stumbled back, blood spilling down the front of his face as Trafalgar rushed him. She knocked him to the ground and turned to the girls.

"Quickly now, ladies!"

Violet waited until both sisters were clear before she followed. The circus was still in full swing, with the gasps and cheers of the crowd serving as a chorus for their escape. They took the same route as the man who had been promised a new car and caught up with him at the main gate. He turned when he heard them approaching and bared his teeth in a snarl.

"Should've known better than to trust a couple of--"

Whatever he'd been about to say was silenced by another swing of Trafalgar's bat. His head snapped back and Trafalgar swept his leg out from under him with a swift kick.

Violet pointed toward where she had parked once they were out of the circus grounds.

Frieda slowed and looked back. "He's holding others..."

"We'll send someone back once we have you to safety," Violet promised. "You're our priority right now."

Neither of the sisters looked happy, but they picked up the pace.

"Stop them!"

Trafalgar clucked her tongue. "A bat to the face doesn't have the stopping power it once did." To Violet, she said, "Get the girls to the car, then come back and get me."

"You'll be all right?" Violet asked.

Trafalgar winked and brushed her wife's hand. "Just come back and get me. I spent a day working alongside these gentlemen. I'm confident I'll still be standing when you get here."

Violet nodded and ushered the Ickes sisters along. Trafalgar stopped running and spun on the ball of one foot until she was facing her pursuers. Three carnies, two of them bearded with blood, were practically tripping over themselves to catch up. As she'd expected from seeing them do hard labor, all three were already gasping for air before they had reached her.

"Shall we call a time-out before we begin, gents?" she asked, relaxing her stance. "I would hate for you to use breathlessness as an excuse for your impending loss."

The lead man had arrived. "Don't... need much to... deal with you!"

He swung and missed, but it brought him close enough for Trafalgar to punch him in the throat. He gagged, and she dropped her hand to the collar of his shirt. She shoved him backward into the second man, pivoted, and kicked the third man in the stomach. He had the wherewithal to grab her foot in an attempt to drop her. She used it to her advantage and leapt, planting her other foot on one of his friends to propel herself higher. The man holding her foot was suddenly burdened with her entire weight and he fell backward.

When they landed, Trafalgar had no choice but to stomp on his chest. He wheezed and curled into a ball as Trafalgar turned to face the other two men. The one on the bottom was unconscious, while the other was still coughing and spitting and trying to catch his breath.

Headlights washed the scene in a pale yellow glow, and Trafalgar backed away from the men toward the car.

"Mr. Valbuena isn't going to take kindly to this!" said the man who was still capable of speaking.

"I have no doubt he'll be very cross indeed." Trafalgar stepped up onto the passenger side runner, holding onto the strut next to the windshield. Violet backed away from the fallen men, so Trafalgar cupped her free hand next to her mouth and raised her voice to be sure they heard her. "If he's ever in London and feels the urge to get revenge, tell him to look up Rhys Tracking and Investigative Services! We'll be happy to hear his complaints."

The men were still crumpled masses in the middle of the road as Violet continued backing away from the scene. Soon they were far enough away that she stopped long enough for Trafalgar to climb into the passenger seat so she wouldn't have to hang on for the entire ride back to the docks. Trafalgar kept the window down and swore she could still hear the big band music playing well after the circus had fallen out of sight.

"You don't *always* have to antagonize them, you know."

They were in bed in their berth aboard the *Skylarker*, about halfway back to London. The Ickes girls had been offered separate rooms, but they requested to stay together insisting they'd been kept apart more than enough over the past few months. Trafalgar had washed up and changed into a night dress, while Violet had opted to lay down naked beside her. For the fifteen minutes before she spoke, she'd been tracing abstract designs on Trafalgar's upper chest.

"How do you mean?" Trafalgar twisted one of Violet's blonde curls around her forefinger so she could let it go and watch it bounce.

Violet adopted a deeper voice and gave each word a bit of swagger. "Next time he's in London, you tell him where he can find us!"

Trafalgar laughed. "I wasn't quite that cowboy."

"You were very cowboy. I know because I found it very arousing." Violet tilted her head up to kiss Trafalgar's chin.

"Oh, is that so? Well, I may have to visit the Wild West more often."

"My heart wouldn't be able to take it. There's a chance Valbuena will do exactly that. Come looking for us."

Trafalgar nodded. "It's a possibility. But given the fact he'll be facing two charges of kidnapping and imprisonment, I doubt he wants to show his face in London any time soon for anything as petty as revenge. He'll stay on the move, where it's more difficult for the authorities to find him. But not impossible. A circus must advertise, after all." She smiled. "I have a feeling Mr. Valbuena will be far too busy running to worry about something as petty as revenge."

"A dangerous game," Violet said. "But I trust you."

Trafalgar shifted on the bed, a silent invitation for Violet to change position as well. Violet did as she intended, lifting up just enough to move on top of Trafalgar. They kissed again, properly and at length. Trafalgar's hands moved under the blankets and began a slow but thorough exploration. She twisted her head to the side and spoke as she kissed her way across Violet's cheek, over the border of her jaw, down to her throat.

"I shall try to be more careful for your benefit, my love."

"See that you do." Violet's voice was soft, distracted, and her fingers tugged at Trafalgar's nightgown in a series of increasingly frustrated plucks. "Why did I ever buy you this blasted thing...?"

"Because you love a challenge."

"Mm."

The problem of the nightgown was quickly solved and, two minutes later, Trafalgar gripped the headboard with both hands, eyes struggling to stay focused on the crown of blonde curls between her thighs. She was losing the battle when there was a knock on the door.

Trafalgar exhaled in frustration even as Violet lifted her head and wiped the back of her hand across her bottom lip. She looked toward the door, then looked at Trafalgar.

"It might be an issue with the girls."

Trafalgar made a noise very much unlike a human sound. Violet pushed herself up and Trafalgar pulled her legs back and put her feet on the floor. She wrapped herself in a robe and went to the door, opening it just wide enough to see who was foolish enough to be interrupting them.

Captain Araminta Crook had the good grace to look ashamed of herself, head down and eyes up, features twisted into a wince that almost looked like a smile.

"Apologies," she said. "I wanted to give you some time to settle in before I disturbed you, and I didn't realize just how settled you were until I had knocked, and then it seemed like it would be even worse to interrupt for no reason..."

"It's fine, Minty..."

"No it's not."

"No, it's not, but it happened and I will try not to hold it against you."

Araminta cleared her throat and stood up straighter. "I was hoping to have a word with you privately."

Trafalgar nodded. She could hear Violet had already gotten out of bed and was in the process of getting dressed.

"Just give us a moment to get decent."

"Actually I just meant you, if that's not too rude. I have no doubt you'll share what we discuss with your lovely wife afterward, but I'd like to keep the initial conversation just between us."

Trafalgar looked into the room. Violet only had on a shirt, her long bare legs stretching out from underneath. Her hair was tangled, and the flush in her cheeks only enhanced her freckles. Trafalgar felt an almost painful longing for her. Violet, unaware of Trafalgar's ogling, just nodded and motioned for her to go as she pulled on a pair of trousers.

"Give me a moment to dress and I'll come find you," Trafalgar said.

"I'll be on the viewing deck, at the windows." She started to leave, then came back. "And, um... give your wife my most *sincere* apologies, hm...?"

Trafalgar smiled as she closed the door on her.

"Everything okay?" Violet asked.

"Uncertain." She threw on a shirt and quickly buttoned it, stepping into a pair of trousers. "Hopefully it won't take too long. I look forward to seeing where you were going with our conversation."

Violet arched an eyebrow. "I intended to make some very strong points."

"Hm." Trafalgar patted Violet's rear end as she headed out.

The viewing deck was a long corridor which ran along the length of the airship's gondola, a wall of windows which looked out over the French coastline. It was night but she could still see the scattered lights of cities far below, and the curling ribbons of smoke rising up from chimneys that indicated people starting their days.

Araminta was waiting, as promised, and she had a bottle of wine balanced on the railing. She was still in her uniform - red leather jacket and tan jodhpurs with knee-length boots - but the jacket was unbuttoned at the collar to reveal a plain white tee-shirt underneath. Her hair was also down, revealing a multitude of thick silver waves that her updo had been struggling to conceal the past few years.

"Drinking on duty, Captain Crook?" Trafalgar chided.

Araminta smiled. "I'm not above it, on occasion. But no, this is for you and Madam Violet as an apology for the interruption."

She took the bottle and examined the label. It was a nice vintage, but not nice enough for her to refuse as being too generous.

"Unnecessary but appreciated nonetheless," Trafalgar said. "I must say I'm intrigued if you have a topic that can't be brought up in front of Violet."

"I'm not sure how sensitive it is, but decided to err on the side of caution." She rested her arms on the railing and looked out the window. "It's regarding Lady Boone."

Trafalgar tensed and joined Araminta at the railing. "I see." She considered her next words very carefully. "Lady Boone and I haven't spoken in quite some time."

"I'm aware. But the thing is, I haven't heard from her in a while, either. It's been over a year since she took advantage of our arrangement."

Trafalgar frowned. "That's peculiar. I haven't heard of her getting up to anything in London, either. She must be doing something to keep busy."

"I would imagine," Araminta said. "I asked around at the Rookery, but none of the other pilots have been charted, either. I tried to call on her a few months ago, but she never responded to my letters and the house seemed abandoned when I visited. I think she must in there."

"She has to leave *sometime*. If just for food."

Araminta shrugged. "I can only report my own experiences. I was also hoping you could provide your own, given that you're both members of the Mnemosyne Society."

"Technically," Trafalgar said. "Dor— Lady Boone hasn't attended any meetings since our partnership collapsed. I assume other members would have spoken up if she'd reached out to any of them, but there hasn't been a peep. Unless they've been instructed not to tell me about it, which has to be a possibility."

"Yes, I gathered it wasn't an especially harmonious parting of the ways. It's one reason I wasn't sure if I should mention her in front of Violet."

Trafalgar shook her head. "It wouldn't have been a problem. I'm not sure I'm the best person to reach out to her. Honestly I think literally anyone would be a better choice."

"I think you're wrong. But someone has to reach out. She's been in a downward spiral for years. You must have noticed. Even when she was still hiring us to go on expeditions, she was a changed woman. Withdrawn, terse, sometimes even rude to the crew. She locked herself in her berth for the duration of the trip and barely spoke three words to me unless it was absolutely necessary. I was... I was actually trying to come up with a way of rescinding my offer of the *Skylarker's* services when she stopped calling."

"You were going to end your arrangement?"

"It wasn't an action I would've taken lightly," Araminta sighed, sounding guilty even though she hadn't gone through with it. "The woman gave me a chance to say goodbye to my wife before she died. That's a kindness I can never repay in full. But for the first time I felt as if she was taking advantage of us. Treating us like servants. She had us traveling all over the world. Russia to drop her off, back a few weeks later to pick her up and take her into the Congo, another retrieval, then to... to... somewhere in the Middle East. She had us covering thousands and miles and barely made eye contact with me while she was aboard. Forget about treating my crew with respect. I can suck it up, but I refuse to let my crew be treated that way."

Trafalgar nodded. "I understand. But I have to admit, I'm shocked Dorothy would be so disrespectful."

"I'm worried about her. She needs someone who cares enough to check in on her, and is strong enough to stay no matter what she does to try to turn you away."

"You have a high opinion of my abilities," Trafalgar said.

"I fear that she's so far gone that you're the only one who even has a chance of getting through to her. She always had a very short list of friends, and an even shorter one of people she trusted with her life. You were engraved on that shorter list, Trafalgar."

"And then the stone it was engraved on was shattered," Trafalgar said. "We've been estranged longer than we were partners. And before that, we considered each other enemies. Seeing me on her front step may only drive her deeper into seclusion."

"That's possible," Araminta admitted. "But at this point I think it's worth trying. She's already falling farther and farther with each passing day. Unless someone reaches out and risks her claws, I fear she'll never find her way back to us."

Trafalgar nodded slowly. "I think I agree. I hope you're right." She shook her head and looked out the window again. "And God help us if you're wrong..."

CHAPTER ONE

SHE DELAYED as long as she could after returning to London before making good on her promise. They returned the Ickes sisters to their family, received payment, and sent word to the Spanish authorities of the crimes committed by Valbuena and his circus. When they received news that the trailers had been raided and seven other kidnapped foreigners were rescued, Trafalgar officially closed the books on that particular assignment and filed it as a complete success. She used a portion of their proceeds to treat Violet to a lavish dinner at her favorite restaurant and spent the rest of the night ravishing her in a fine hotel that overlooked the Thames.

Violet had stood at the window wrapped in a sheet, sipping at a glass of Araminta's wine, and Trafalgar got out of bed to embrace her from behind. Violet had sagged against her and Trafalgar comfortably accepted the weight against her chest.

"I can't afford to give you this view all the time," Trafalgar said, "but you have my word that I'll show it to you every single time it's within my power."

"There's another view I like much better." Violet turned in her wife's arms. "And you can give it to me for free."

Trafalgar smiled, kissed her, and pulled her back to the bed.

On a Monday morning after their celebrations were over, and after confirming their agency had no outstanding business to occupy her afternoon, Trafalgar reluctantly decided the time had come to pay a visit to Threadneedle Street.

It would be her first trip there in seven years. She'd avoided the entire neighborhood as much as possible, often choosing alternate routes if the more direct path took her too close to familiar streets. She was doing her best to forget that relatively brief period of her life. There were good times... *such* good times, and wonderful memories... but the way it had all crashed down at the end made even those painful to revisit.

Her desk faced Violet's, and she was well aware that her wife had been silently observing her while they ate lunch. She finally turned and met her gaze.

"I can go with you," Violet offered without waiting for Trafalgar to speak what was on her mind. "I'll stay out of sight around the corner so she won't know I'm there, but I can be moral support."

"Thank you, but I think I need to go alone." She sighed and stood up. She looked at Violet again, suddenly hopeful. "Unless she happens to not be home right now."

Violet smiled and shook her head. "Sorry, love. Lady Boone is currently at her home address, on Threadneedle Street."

"Damn." Trafalgar took a deep breath and let it out. She squared her shoulders and took her jacket from the back of the chair. "I've faced a minotaur, I can handle an awkward conversation."

"Huzzah," Violet said.

Trafalgar stepped around their desks and bent down to kiss Violet. "I won't be long. I hope."

"I shall await your report."

With nothing else to prevent her departure, Trafalgar left.

Their office was in Marylebone between a pub and an optician. Their flat was just a few blocks away above a tailor. Violet was responsible for finding both, even if her ability hadn't quite been powerful enough to respond to "find us a storefront and a place to live within our meager budget." Even without using her shortcut, Violet was adept at the old-fashioned kind of detective work and quickly found the perfect location for them to set up their shingle.

Once they had the office, it was relatively easy to find an affordable living space nearby. The two-room flat was by no means equal to the Threadneedle townhouse Trafalgar had grown used to, but she'd never required anything quite that fancy anyway. As long as she had Violet with her, any space would have felt like a mansion.

While waiting for the bus, she tried to think of what she was going to say. When she boarded and took her seat, she whispered a speech under her breath to prepare herself for saying it out loud. When she disembarked over a trip that was much shorter than she'd hoped, she walked slowly and hoped for an epiphany.

The words never came. She ended up standing on the sidewalk and looking up at a door that had once led to home, her sanctuary, the place where she had discovered secrets of the world and the truth about herself.

She finally decided she had delayed as long as she possibly could. She climbed the front steps and her hand automatically reached for the knob. She stopped herself at the last second, curling her fingers into her palm to form a fist. She knocked, took a step back, and waited. A minute passed. She pursed her lips and looked over her shoulder at the street. No one seemed to be paying her much attention yet, but she was certain that would change if she lingered. She knocked again, harder this time.

If Violet hadn't confirmed she was home, Trafalgar would have taken the coward's retreat and claimed she'd tried her best. But she knew the truth and couldn't feign ignorance, so she knocked a third time and waited two more minutes before she decided a different tactic was required.

She returned to the street and looked back at the building. The alleyway between the townhouse and its neighbor was blocked by a brick wall taller than Trafalgar was. A quick look around didn't reveal anything she could easily use as a stepping stone. She could break one of the curtained windows on the ground floor, but that was certain to draw the police on a street so overrun by banks and bankers. There was a chance she could climb onto the window and use that to clamber over the alley wall, but it would be enormously difficult to do that without attracting attention.

She was wasting time on schemes. The street wasn't crowded with people, but it also wasn't abandoned, and any attempts she made at breaking-and-entering was bound to raise a ruckus. The color of her skin would remove the benefit of any doubts the constables might have, and she couldn't count on the owner of the house to vouch for her in the event of an arrest.

Trafalgar looked at the door again, and a stupid thought occurred to her. "No," she whispered. Then she tilted her head to the side and arched an eyebrow. "But you know Violet will scold you mercilessly if you don't try. And she *will* ask..."

She climbed the stairs again. This time she didn't stop herself from taking the knob as if she was an invited guest. She twisted, the knob turned without hesitation, and she pushed the door open.

"For pity's sake," she muttered.

She stepped inside and closed the door behind her. The foyer was cold, and the rooms facing the front of the street were so heavily curtained that it could have been the dead of night beyond their thresholds. She ventured toward the kitchen and craned her neck. She could smell a funk on the air, some rotting thing, and she decided that part of the house could wait until later to be explored. She went to the foot of the stairs and looked up.

"Hello? Is anyone here?" She rested her hand on the banister, then lifted it and saw her palm had left an imprint in the dust that had gathered there. "Lord, how have you been living like this?" she said under her breath.

"Trafalgar?"

She startled at the voice and looked back at the second floor landing. The woman standing there was dressed in trousers and a sleeveless undershirt, her hair thick and wild and hanging around her head like wild vines. Due to those tangles, it would have been difficult to make out her features even without the shadows, but there was no mistaking her stance. The name she'd struggled so hard not to say over the past seven years fell past her lips almost before it appeared in her mind.

"Dorothy."

"What are you doing here?"

Trafalgar tried to tamp down the unease she felt. This was Dorothy Boone, Lady Boone, a woman she had called a rival, enemy, friend, colleague, and lover, and not always in that order. No matter what had passed between them, she considered herself closer to this woman than anyone else, bar Violet, and yet her brain and tongue refused to cooperate. She felt awkward and terrified at the thought of actually speaking with her.

"Never mind," Dorothy said, just as Trafalgar was about to force words from her mouth. She turned and walked away from the landing. "We have so much to discuss. I was just thinking about contacting you." She didn't bother to raise her voice as she entered her office. "It's been... it's been a while, hasn't it? I'm not sure. It feels like it's been a very long time. A year? God, tell me it hasn't been a year since we spoke."

Trafalgar ascended to the top of the stairs so she could hear Dorothy without straining. "It's been considerably longer than a year, Lady Boone."

"I was afraid of that." Dorothy was by her desk staring down at the mess of papers scattered across it. "Well, it's no matter now. We have so much to discuss." She started to clear the mess, then looked up with a furrowed brow. "Did I already say that?"

"Yes," Trafalgar said.

"Crumbs. These days I can't keep always track of what's..." She tapped her temple. "And what's..." She drew a straight line out from her lips.

"Are you all right, Lady Boone?"

"Lady Boone," Dorothy mumbled under her breath, sounding even more confused. "Lady Boone, Lady Boone. What's all that about, hm? You keep calling me Lady Boone. What happened to Dorothy?"

"I'm... I don't..." She took a breath. "Dorothy. When was the last time you spoke with anyone?"

Dorothy considered the question, head turned slightly toward the curtained window as if she could see out of it. Finally she gave up and flipped her hands.

"I don't know. From this time? In this line? Not counting then? Ages."

"And the house..." Trafalgar turned and gestured, then held up her dusty hand. "It looks as if it's been abandoned. I think I smelled rotting food down in the kitchen. Have you been living here this entire time?"

"Where else would I live? This is my home. God, I'm thirsty." She opened one of the desk drawers as if it held a glass of water. Finding none, she shot to her feet again and marched past Trafalgar. "First I will get some water and then we will talk. Over a year, you said? That can't be right. But I doubt you'd lie about something like that." She moved down the stairs at a quick pace, and Trafalgar was forced to keep up with her. "What has been keeping you busy over the past however long it's been?"

"There were, ah, quite a few people who retained powers after the, um, incident. Violet and I have been doing our best to find them so we can~"

"Violet!" Dorothy turned and grabbed Trafalgar's shoulders.

They were in the hallway that led to the kitchen. Dorothy was smiling broadly, her eyes wide behind the hanging strands of her hair. "You're still with Violet? What *wonder*-ful news! Are you still courting one another?"

"We've... we're... m-married..."

Dorothy's lips parted in a gasp. "Married! Trafalgar... ah... crumbs. I can't think of her surname."

"Rhys."

"Trafalgar Rhys." She clapped her hands on Trafalgar's shoulders. "Wonderful! What a wonderful ring it has to it. I'm so pleased for you."

Trafalgar reached up and removed Dorothy's hands from her as gently as she could. "Dorothy, I'm here because I'm concerned for you. A lot of us are. And to be honest, seeing you this way has only heightened my concern."

"What way?"

"Are you mad? Your clothes are filthy. Your *house* is filthy. You're speaking without taking a breath, bouncing from one topic to the next. What in the would have *you* been up to in this house for the past seven years?"

Dorothy took a step back, suddenly sobered. "Did you just say *seven* years...? *Seven?*"

"Yes."

"No, that's not possible. That would make it 1930."

"September."

"No." The word was a breath, and Dorothy stumbled back as if she was ducking it. "No, it couldn't be that long. Could it?" She looked down at the floor and her hair fell across her face, obscuring her features again. "1930... a whole new decade. Hah. Trafalgar, married... One decade to another. Skipping an entire span. Time marching on." She straightened suddenly and used both hands to rake the hair out of her face.

"I'm sorry to have told you that way," Trafalgar said, still unsure if she believed the date was a revelation. "It was cruel of me..."

"No, no, it's not unreasonable to assume someone has a basic grasp of what year it is. I'm the one who should be apologizing to you. I haven't been entirely honest with you." She held out her hand. Trafalgar looked at it and then, after a moment, extended her hand to take it. Dorothy squeezed her fingers. "I've been working on a single project, but I think I've finally cracked it. You've come on a very good day, Miss Trafa~ Mrs. Rhys. All the answers are within my grasp, I just have to arrange them. And when I do... when I do, when I'm ready, things are going to be *very* different indeed."

Trafalgar said, "What exactly are you planning, Dorothy?"

Dorothy smiled, and Trafalgar was alarmed to see the manic energy sparking in them again.

"I'm going to bring her back. I know how to bring back Beatrice. And if you're willing to help me, she can be back with us by this time tomorrow."

She laughed and stepped closer, kissed Trafalgar's cheek, and gave her hand a final squeeze before letting it go.

"I'm really so glad you're here today. It's perfect. It's fate."

Dorothy laughed, turned, and practically skipped into the kitchen. Trafalgar watched her go and then, with a heavy sigh, followed after her.

She found Dorothy examining the cabinets with a perplexed, disgusted expression on her face.

"What do you mean you can bring Beatrice back? She's gone, Dorothy."

"That's not exactly true. She was never exactly *gone*, not in the way most people are. Not the way Desmond is. But if this works, then maybe we can find a way to make amends for that as well." She gave a sharp laugh and picked up a molded loaf of bread. "Good lord. Perhaps I can order someone to bring me food. Honestly, nothing here can be safe to eat."

Trafalgar cleared her throat. "Yes, the smell would attest to that fact. Come with me, Dorothy. Come to my home. You can eat something... bathe. Rest."

"Give my congratulations to your wife?" Dorothy winked. "Honestly, I'm so happy for you. I don't even mind that I wasn't invited to your wedding. Was there a wedding?"

"No, we~"

"Oh, that makes sense. Well, it's fine then. You should have given me the opportunity to send a gift, however. I must make amends for that once this whole mess is settled."

Trafalgar said, "Right. Of course. Do you want to... to change into something a bit more appropriate before we leave? Maybe pack a bag? We don't have much room but we'd be more than happy to have you for as long as you need."

"Have me? Why would I need to stay with you? This is my house.

And yes, it's a bit..." She made a noise of disgust. "But open a few windows, run a duster over a few things, visit the market, it'll be right as rain in no time."

"Dorothy, you're not well."

"I'm perfectly fine."

"You have no food!" Trafalgar was practically shouting. "You look disheveled. Your clothing is soiled, your hair is a rat's nest. Frankly, I have no idea how you've been living here all this time."

Dorothy blinked at her. "Lord. I haven't been *living* here. No one could live in these conditions."

"You... but..." Trafalgar's anger was replaced with confusion. "Then where have you been living?"

"Nineteen-ten."

Trafalgar didn't comprehend. "Nineteen-ten what? Is there a street address?"

"The year of our Lord, nineteen hundred and ten. August and September, to be exact."

Trafalgar's shoulders sagged. "You've lost your senses."

Dorothy shook her head. "No. No, I knew you would say that." She reached into the pocket of her slacks and withdrew a much-folded sheet of paper. She held it out to Trafalgar. "I bought that paper two days ago, brand-new. Look. It's not even yellowed."

The paper did look new. It was dated October 3, 1910. Trafalgar skimmed the articles and then looked at Dorothy skeptically.

"You could have gotten this anywhere..."

"I got it from a newsstand not far from the hotel where I was staying. I wanted to stay in this house... God, it was hard not to drop by and see my grandmother. But I wanted to make sure I didn't impact history any more than I had by just being there." She held up a finger when Trafalgar started to speak. "And don't you dare claim time travel doesn't exist. We've both seen the proof of it. The Mnemosyne Society is mostly funded by money that came from a woman who hasn't even been born yet. You and I saw the proof with our own eyes in South America. That airplane! The fact that a handful of days were completely rewritten by our actions in that cavern. I traveled in time, Trafalgar. Obviously I need to get a little better about proper aiming... I should have been back months ago."

Trafalgar decided against trying to convince Dorothy she was delusional and opted to move forward.

"Okay, let's assume you did go back in time to 1910. Why would you... for what purpose..."

"To find some way out of this mess. Magic, elementals. We let the genie out of the bottle for the Great War, Trafalgar, and nothing we did was ever going to put it back in. We were careening toward a cliff and the only way to change course is to go back and never get in the car in the first place."

Trafalgar pulled a chair away from the dinner table and sat down. "You want to change history."

Dorothy sat down as well. "We know that magic experienced a resurgence during the War. Very powerful practitioners in a relatively small area created a weak spot in the fabric of reality. Magic started seeping back into this plane. We tried to stop that leak from becoming a flood, but everything we did only seemed to make the problem worse.

"So I started thinking. Magic had to be coming from somewhere, yes? So I spent a lot of time exploring theories, chasing down scholars, finding out every possible explanation for where it might originate. I never found a solid answer but it led me to another question that is equally intriguing." She leaned closer. "We dedicated our lives to exploring lost civilizations. Entire groups of people who lived on this planet and then just vanished without a trace. Monsters and wizards and superpowers who ruled the globe only to be forgotten in a handful of generations. Where did they go? How did they die out?"

Trafalgar had to admit she was curious. "And what did you discover?"

"Magic is a plague, Trafalgar. Not a plague of illness, but one of pure joy, bliss, power. Magic gives people whatever they want. And quite often, what people want is what other people have. Magic enabled horrific wars, atrocities that would never have been possible otherwise, gave madmen the ability to grind their enemies into dust, and allowed retribution from their enemies in turn. It was a vicious cycle that left the world scrubbed clean.

"And once its work was done, magic went dormant. It lay waiting for the next superpower, for the next fool hungry for power or infamy, and it began infecting them."

Trafalgar said, "That's a bold claim."

"It makes sense. Trust me. I've spent a long time on this. And then, last month... no, I suppose... I suppose now it was over a year ago. Hm." She shook her head. "I got my hands on an artifact which would allow me to travel in time. I thought if I went back before the

War began, I could find a way to somehow stop it from happening. It did not go well." She looked down at her hands for a moment before she waved away the memory. "But I consider it a victory because I proved it's possible. I know what I must do now, and I have everything I need to make things right."

"Think about what you're saying, Dorothy. It's madness. Think of the consequences of what you're proposing. Taking away magic could cause the war to stretch on for another year, another decade. Thousands more lives, millions potentially, could be lost."

"Or magic caused the war to drag on longer than necessary. If we take away the most powerful weapon we had at our disposal, maybe everyone would have been less willing to fight. The war could end after one year, and millions of lives will be *saved*."

"A possibility," Trafalgar admitted. "But the fact that we just don't know should be giving you pause. We can't in good conscience roll the dice on something that would absolutely change the course of the entire world just to save one person, no matter how precious she was to us. You're allowing your grief and your pain to blind your common sense. Please. Come to my home. Rest."

Dorothy shook her head and stood up. "I can't. I've wasted far too much time already, and I just lost an entire year. I have to put things into motion."

Trafalgar stood as well. "Dorothy, after everything I've seen... the state of the house, your current dishevelment, I'm afraid I must insist. Your friends are concerned for your mental state. And even you have to admit that since Beatrice's death, you've completely changed. You're in a spiral."

"I'm not," Dorothy said. "I have been focused. Do you and the rest of the society expect me to sit in my office and draw maps all day, or crawl around in tombs gathering dusty artifacts, when there's a chance Beatrice can be saved? Frankly, I'm offended you're going on with your life as if she meant nothing to you."

"My heart aches for Beatrice," Trafalgar said, pushing back her anger at Dorothy's implication. "But the fact remains that she is gone. Nothing we do can bring her back. It's madness to try. Either you come home with me so Violet and I can help you recover, or we will begin arrangements to confine you to an institution where~"

Dorothy barked a laugh. "You'll have me committed!"

Trafalgar held up her hands. "We'll coordinate with Cora. She institutionalized herself for a time so she could overcome a powerful grief, do you remember? It did wonders for her and I believe you would greatly benefit from the same time away."

"Get out of my house."

"Dorothy~"

Dorothy picked up the closest thing to hand, which happened to be a plate. She hurled it at Trafalgar, who smacked it to the floor. It shattered between them.

"Leave this house at once, Trafalgar, or I shall be forced to... I will..." She squeezed her eyes shut. "I-I will be forced to use force."

"Dorothy," Trafalgar said softly. "You're clearly not well. A grief this powerful can alter your memories. Can make you think you had impossible experiences. Such as traveling in time..."

This time Dorothy took a moment to find a weapon and found a knife sitting on the counter. She swung the blade around, forcing Trafalgar to back up a step. Trafalgar stared at her in disbelief.

"You can't be serious."

"I have asked you politely to leave. I am prepared to be much less friendly. Go! If you will not help me, there's no need for me to ever see your face again. And tell the rest of the fucking Society that the same goes for all of them as well. None of them lifted a finger to help me save Trix, and I'll be damned before I suffer any of their pity."

Trafalgar backed out of the kitchen and into the hallway. She held her hands up, palm out. "We love you, Dorothy. We're concerned for you."

"Then be concerned from a distance." She followed Trafalgar down the hall, using the knife like a lead. "When Beatrice comes back, and she *will* be coming back, mark my words... I will invite you back so you may beg for her forgiveness. Until then, you are not welcome in this house, or anywhere that happens to be in front of my fucking face."

"We want to help you," Trafalgar said. "If we must do that against your will, so be it."

"A threat?"

"One you will thank us for when you're... yourself again."

Dorothy's lips pulled back to expose her teeth. "Leave, or bleed."

Trafalgar opened the door and stepped outside. "We won't give up on you, Dorothy."

"You already have."

Dorothy slammed the door in her face.

CHAPTER TWO

OF COURSE there was a chance that Trafalgar was right.

Dorothy stood in the front hall for a long time, resting her head against the door with the knife at her side. She'd just brandished a knife against Trafalgar. That was certainly the act of a madwoman, wasn't it? She waited until her breathing was steady before she risked peeking out the window. The street in front of the townhouse was empty save for a few bankers passing by. Dorothy took a deep breath and exhaled it, then left the front hall to return the knife to the drawer.

The house was an absolute wreck. She couldn't deny that, either. But that had to be proof of what had really happened. There's no way she'd been living here. The food was spoiled, everything was rimed with dust, and there was no evidence anyone had been sleepwalking through the corridors having an extremely vivid hallucination.

She went upstairs and into her bedroom. The bed was made, the curtains pulled tight around its four-poster frame. The air felt still and undisturbed.

"Well, Trix? Is she right? Am I delusional?"

Dorothy went to the vanity and sat down. She wiped away the dust which had accumulated on the mirror and saw herself.

"Good lord, no wonder Trafalgar wants to lock me up."

She plucked at the wild strands of her hair and then used both hands to push it away from her face. Her roots were mostly white now, a change she'd been aware of but found easy enough to ignore while she focused on her mission. She was supposed to be immortal. That was the threat Riya Lennox hurled at her. Was she going to live forever only as an old, wrinkled crone? It was a question for another time, she decided. For now there were only two options. She could start going to great lengths to conceal the color, or she could embrace the change.

She opened the drawers of the vanity until she found a pair of silver shears. She leaned forward in the chair and began cutting before she could overthink it.

A year. She had been gone for a *year*. The man who had pointed her toward the artifact warned that it wouldn't be precise, but she'd never imagined such a huge gap. Especially when she had arrived within a few days of her target in 1910. She was supposed to be able to come back within moments of leaving no matter how much time she spent in the past and she'd gotten sloppy.

Red hairs cascaded down in front of her as she continued to cut. She didn't bother much with style, but she did try to keep her cuts as straight as possible. She wanted it short, but not too short. Nothing too radical.

Before going back in time, she spent six years chasing every possible myth or rumor about the elementals in preparation for the trip. She interrogated the Dov until the woman had finally banned Dorothy from ever crossing into her territory again. "You know more about the elementals than I do at this point," the Dov had said. "I've done all I can for you. But I do wish you luck."

Dorothy had trekked all over the world to the places the other elementals had originated. It took her two months to find the remote Russian village where Oksana Vengerov, the fire elemental, was from. No one could provide her with any information, but she spent a week there asking questions anyway. She discovered that Oksana kept to herself and rarely interacted with anyone. "But the last few winters," an old woman finally told her, "we found glowing stones in the forest. They burned as if lit from within. Just one could keep an entire house warm until dawn. I don't know what we're going to do without her..."

From there she went to the Belgian Congo and found Kumona Majambu's home. The people who had once been Kumona's friends and neighbors were naturally protective of her and it took Dorothy over a month to gain their trust. When they finally talked, they confirmed that Kumona's abilities only manifested a few years earlier when the last water elemental, Emmeline Potter, was killed. In the brief time she had them, however, she used her control of water to provide everyone in the area with fresh drinking water, frequent rainstorms, and irrigation for their crops. They knew she was gone, and they were deeply concerned about their future. Dorothy left them with a promise she would do everything possible to find out if Kumona was truly gone for good.

Her final stop was Persia, the homeland of the wind elemental Nasim Turan. The first time she mentioned Nasim's name, the man she was speaking to immediately turned his back and retreated as fast as possible without actually running. She was kicked out of restaurants, had her feet spit on, and cursed out in at least two different languages before she decided to try a different tact. She asked a store clerk about wind spirits. The clerk crossed herself, but answered.

"We were cursed to have one in our midst. Djinn. A demon of sand and fire brought to life by the winds. We banished her from town, but we could see her out on the dunes. Watching us. Waiting for someone to slip up and invite her in. Before she was possessed, she was just like any of us. When she changed..." The woman shivered and waved her hand, dismissing the entire conversation. "Do not ask about this. No one will speak to you."

Dorothy decided that much was clear, so she cut her losses and headed back home. She locked herself in the berth aboard the *Skylarker* and tried to write down everything she knew about the elementals and their myths. It was difficult to focus with Araminta's persistent invitations to dinner or to go out and look at the stars or some other blasted waste of time. She wanted to explain but didn't want to risk confusing herself before she'd lined everything up in her mind. Trying to tell someone else would tangle the strings that were already fairly twisted and knotted up.

The four elementals came together to create a void which effectively quashed magic not just in London, but around the world. The years leading up to 1923 were full of stories about a resurgence in magical abilities. More and more people were finding themselves able to do remarkable things, like Violet Rhys' ability to find anything in the world. At first she was trying to find a way to fix that moment, to undo their sacrifice, but then she realized she was coming at it backwards.

She needed to make their sacrifice unnecessary.

Her first jaunt to 1910 had been a test to see if it was really possible. Now she knew that it was, even if returning was a bit trickier than she'd like. She had observed the Great War from both sides, the beginning and the end, and she had a good idea of why and how magic was first utilized in battle. She knew the players involved. She knew she could stop them, convince them to try another tactic. If she was successful, it would change everything.

Dorothy stopped cutting and ran her hand through her hair. It was mannishly short, a combination of red and silver. It was a lovely look, if she did say so herself, and she put the scissors down before she was tempted to do more.

Awakening magic had been the cause of so much pain in her life. Losing Beatrice, obviously, but it would also potentially protect Desmond from his own untimely demise. She could put so many things right. She could remake the world the way it was supposed to be, and wasn't that a noble pursuit? Yes, the war might run on, more people might die, but that wouldn't be her fault. Not if the end result was a brighter, better world. Otherwise, what were they fighting for in the first place?

She stood up and brushed the clippings from her lap and blouse. Her clothes really were filthy. She stripped them off and went to the washroom. She cleaned herself up, scrubbing hard to get some of the more stubborn dirt from her arms and face.

One of her goals in the past had been to determine if her memory would be altered when she changed history. She remembered visiting Big Ben with her grandmother around that time and knew it would be the perfect test. It was one of her fondest memories. She lay in wait outside the townhouse and watched the older woman leave, a young girl trotting along beside her. Dorothy deeply regretted that she might taint such a happy memory, but it had to be something that would definitely stick in her young mind.

She had pulled a kerchief up over her lower face, tucked her hair under a flat cap, and charged out after the pair. She was dressed like a man, all her clothes oversized, and Eula Boone heard her coming just before she reached them.

"Ruffian!" her grandmother had said.

Dorothy snatched the purse from Eula's hand, pivoted on the ball of her foot, and used her shoulder to shove her younger self to the ground. She ducked just in time to avoid the swing of Eula's walking stick. Eula had taught Dorothy how to fight, and she knew all the old woman's moves. She avoided another swing, hunched her shoulders, and ran as fast as she could to duck around the corner.

She ran until she was positive Eula hadn't pursued her. Confident she'd gotten away, she purchased a large box and put Eula's handbag inside. She had to take a few coins from the purse to ship it, but she hoped her grandmother would consider it worth the price to have her things back.

That night, Dorothy lay in bed and tried to remember that day. She remembered the walk along the Thames to Westminster. It was nearly two hours, and her grandmother had bought them both ice creams at a little shop they passed. No. She tilted her head to the side. No, they hadn't been able to stop because...

Dorothy had suddenly remembered the terror, the tall and gangly man who had shoved her to the ground and stolen her grandmother's purse. She remembered the odd way he fled, her mind filled with images of Spring-Heeled Jack or some other inhuman monster. She remembered Eula helping her up, dusting her off, and saying, "Well, we're lucky that walking is free."

"And so is looking," Dorothy had said.

But no. She also remembered the ice cream. It was rich and delicious, and she remembered how sticky her hands had been when her grandmother explained what Parliament was about. She remembered it as a perfectly ordinary, perfectly beautiful day. But she also remembered the one tainted by theft. She also remembered a few days later when a box arrived containing Eula's purse. The only thing missing was the price of postage.

"How utterly queer," Eula muttered.

As far as Dorothy knew, the mystery had never been solved. Of course now she knew. Now she knew everything.

She could change the past, and her own memories would remain unaffected.

Her months in 1910 had been harrowing, invigorating, and educational in ways she hadn't anticipated. She was essentially homeless in that era. No resources, no contacts or savings, not even a friend where she could beg sanctuary. The Dorothy Boone of that time was a child, and she couldn't reach out to her grandmother without risking damage to the timeline. Of course her entire goal was to damage the timeline, but preferably not to her own history.

But her history would be changed, wouldn't it? Irrevocably. She stopped buttoning her blouse, fingers hovering over a button as her mind put the pieces together. She and Trafalgar were rivals until the Weeks brothers inadvertently brought them together by trying to assassinate them both. If the Weeks had no need to find the Minotaur, Trafalgar would never have been anything but an enemy to her.

"No," Dorothy muttered, and resolutely continued buttoning her blouse. She muttered to thin air, as if she was still arguing with Trafalgar. "I will remember what we once had. And I can explain to her that we gain more as allies than as enemies. She will understand. Her friends will also be alive. She will see that I was right all along."

She nodded once, agreeing with herself.

She looked in the mirror and smoothed down the front of her blouse.

She would succeed. Anything that changed for the worst, she could simply put right again. She and Trafalgar would be partners once again, and Beatrice would be alive. There was just one more thing she had to do in the present-day, one task left before her plan was complete and she could finally put her plan into motion. It would be difficult, but time was of the essence. She had to move quickly.

It was time to get started.

Though the Mnemosyne Society had grown in both membership and wealth over the past few years, the members still considered the Inkwell to be their main base of operations. The upstairs was now home to their most valuable books and artifacts, a veritable museum of the uncanny. They had vastly increased security measures in accordance with the items kept within its walls, but they maintained the ground floor's aesthetic as a pub.

Trafalgar called Violet from the Inkwell's office and asked her to get in touch with the rest of the council, their name for the founding members of the society. She estimated it would be an hour before everyone showed up, so she had that long to explain what had happened with Dorothy and what needed to be done going forward.

The problem was that Trafalgar couldn't say with any confidence what exactly had happened. If Dorothy was delusional, she absolutely needed to be somewhere she could be observed and looked after. If the entire time travel scenario was a hallucination, she needed medical attention and she needed it as soon as possible. But if it was true... if Dorothy really had traveled in time, and if she intended to do it again, she was dangerous. She posed a threat to the entire planet, and they would have to look put aside any friendship or loyalty they had for her and do the difficult thing for the greater good.

Cora Hyde and Violet arrived together, deep in conversation as they came into the building. Trafalgar left the office to greet then, and Cora turned worried eyes on her.

"Violet was just telling me you spoke with Dorothy. That must have been quite interesting."

"That's one word for it," Trafalgar said.

The door opened again and Susannah Bird entered. Trafalgar tensed at the sight of her, even though she knew the woman's rough edges had been sanded off long ago. She was one of Maud Keaton's most trusted associates when she was still one of the Forty Elephants. She'd been willing to commit murder at Keaton's order, and had no qualms about breaking any number of more minor offenses. But in the past few years, during her apprenticeship with the Keepings, she'd become a respectable member of the Society and was someone Agnes and Leonard trusted above almost anyone else. She had started serving as their proxy when they were unable to attend meetings. That alone was enough to make Trafalgar upset by her arrival.

"Agnes?" she guessed.

Susannah nodded. "Quite weak, of late. Leonard's watching over her, but more often than not, we have to nursemaid both of 'em."

Trafalgar twisted her lips. Agnes and Leonard Keeping had been at the forefront of the adventuring community for decades. They were highly respected and even now, Trafalgar would have hesitated to bet against them in a physical altercation. But there was no denying they were growing weaker with every passing year and soon they would have to officially give their position in the Society's council to Susannah.

Cora shook her head. "I suppose in our line of work, being allowed to pass away quietly in your own bed is a sort of blessing. Heaven knows they deserve it."

"I concur. But hopefully it is a blessing they won't be given for quite some time yet. They've also earned a peaceful retirement."

Susannah said, "On that note, I've been given authority to sit in for them at this meeting of the Society. Are we all here? Shall we begin?"

"We're still waiting for Cecil's representative."

Cora and Susannah both rolled their eyes, and Violet grimaced.

Trafalgar pressed her lips together and checked her watch. It was still before their arranged meeting time, but the fact that whoever Cecil sent would be the last to arrive was simply typical of his nature.

To his credit, Cecil had also grown much more respectable in the past few years. He took charge of ten apprentices, all former Elephants, and promised to do everything he could to put them on the straight and narrow. From what Trafalgar could tell, he had a very broad definition of that term. There were rumors among the others that his ladies still engaged in the occasional con job or heist, though there was little to no concrete evidence against them.

Trafalgar and Violet had tried to keep an eye on him, but he resented what he called "your blasted mother-henning" and created a North American branch of the Mnemosyne Society in New York. His reasoning was that history was happening all over the world, and it didn't make sense for their very large group to remain centered in a very tiny city. As much as Trafalgar hated to admit it, he had a point. A North America base was a good idea and had proven valuable several times since he set it up. She was still very uncomfortable that he was so far away and impossible to monitor.

Then there was the matter of how he was represented in these meetings given the fact he was on another continent. It was... unsettling, to say the least.

Trafalgar was just beginning to brace herself for the sight when she heard footsteps coming from the back room. Everyone turned toward the door and waited as the slow, lumbering stomps grew louder. After a full minute, the door swung open and something that looked like a man joined them. His torso was a solid block wrapped in fabric, his arms and legs thick trunks, and his head was a stone with the barest hint of a face drawn onto it. It stood, silent and insensate as a statue, in the corner of the back room when it wasn't in use.

Edith Bowles, one of Cecil's apprentices, could create golems, animated creatures that could be controlled from afar. Somehow this golem had been enchanted with a link to Cecil so he could manipulate it whenever he wished. He saw whatever it saw, he heard whatever was said in its presence. The only good thing about the monster was that it wasn't able to speak.

"You're late," Trafalgar said, even though that wasn't strictly true. "If you try to blame it on the time difference again, I'll be forced to assume you're unable to understand simple arithmetic and cease inviting you to any meetings set during the daylight hours. Am I understood?"

The Cecil golem nodded. Somehow she could sense him rolling his eyes an ocean away.

"Very well." She gestured at the booths and the others took their seats, turning to face outward. The golem remained standing because it physically couldn't sit down.

Trafalgar stood in front of the bar, arms crossed over her chest. She held her breath, hoping it would freeze the moment in time, prevent her from saying what needed to be said. She'd grown to love this room. Every booth had a tall wooden back, separating each table from its neighbors to provide a bit of privacy. The large windows that faced west lit up like crystal every night when the sun began setting and everything in the room glowed and grew long shadows. At the moment she could see a few cobwebs in the corners and dust motes swirling in the sunbeams.

She sensed her audience was growing restless, so she released the breath and said the words she'd been trying to hold back. "We need to discuss our Lady Boone problem."

Susannah took a breath and let it out slowly. "Well, thank goodness for that. Agnes keeps asking after her, but it didn't seem like something I should bring up."

"You mentioned you spoke to her," Cora said, for the benefit of the new arrivals.

Trafalgar nodded. "Unfortunately, yes. I'm not entirely sure how much of what she said should be taken at face value. She claims that she traveled twenty years back in time to explore the possibility of changing history."

Cora and Violet exchanged looks. Susannah raised an eyebrow. "Well, that's not possible."

"Ah," Trafalgar said, holding her hands up as if weighing the debate. "Lady Boone and I have first-hand evidence that it might actually be possible under the correct circumstances. We can't take that as definitive proof that she's telling the truth, but we also can't dismiss it outright."

"If she didn't travel in time, it's still a delicate issue," Cora said. "We have to determine if she is deliberately lying or if she is having a delusion."

Trafalgar said, "Precisely. Even without knowing for certain what she's been through the past few months, action must be taken before she harms herself or causes irreparable damage to the world."

Susannah said, "What do you suggest?"

"I haven't a clue. I'm sorry, I wish I could be of more help, but the two of us have been estranged for too long. The brief conversation we had today at her townhouse resulted in threats and violence. I'm afraid we can't approach her as friends."

Cora sat up straighter. "Are... I'm sorry, are you suggesting we treat her as an enemy?"

"I believe it's the only way to get through to her. In the end, it doesn't matter what the truth is. Either she intends to go back in time and change history, or it's a fantasy she concocted in her head. Our imperative in both cases is the same. We must prevent her from acting, and she's made it clear that she won't listen to reason."

She sighed and closed her eyes.

"As of today and until further notice, Lady Dorothy Boone is to be considered an enemy of the Mnemosyne Society."

CHAPTER THREE

THEY SPENT the rest of the afternoon planning their attack. Everyone in the room was aware of how sly and crafty Dorothy could be in a fight. They would have to be precise in their movements and completely in charge of the entire situation. If they allowed her to get the upper hand, the whole endeavor would be for naught.

"We must treat her as we would any other threat," Trafalgar reminded them. "Once we have her secure, and we're certain she's not a threat to herself or others, we can work on making apologies."

Only a handful of the new Mnemosyne members had retained their magically-granted abilities, but those few had spent the intervening years becoming adept at their skills. Violet, of course, was still a finder. Florence Barbour could still duplicate herself, though she could only a handful of dupes at a time and even that left her exhausted. Alma Jessup could pass through solid walls and doors. Isabella Stannard's skin was as unbreakable as always, and Zilla Beverly could shoot out projectiles with tips that excreted a sedative. Those women were going to be key to the plan to subdue Dorothy, and Susannah volunteered to gather them.

"We're losing daylight quickly," Trafalgar said with a look toward the window. "I would greatly prefer not to attack the Threadneedle house at night. Darkness will be a benefit to her. She's already got far too many advantages for my tastes."

Cora said, "It's going to be all of us against her. Surely the odds will be on our side."

Trafalgar raised an eyebrow. "You've been her friend longer than any of us. Do you truly believe Dorothy Boone will be overwhelmed by mere numbers?"

Cora twisted her lips. "A valid point..."

"Mm."

Trafalgar drew up a floorplan of the house and used matchsticks to represent each member of the raiding party. First they would have Violet confirm Dorothy was still there before they did anything, as there was little point in breaching the house if she'd already headed out. Assuming she was present, Trafalgar would go to the door with Isabella and Zilla. Isabella would act as a human shield just in case Dorothy was prepared for an assault. Trafalgar would give her one final chance to see reason and come with them. If she refused, Zilla would sedate her.

"Surely she'll have anticipated that," Cora said.

"Of course she will," Trafalgar admitted. "The problem with going up against a friend and ally is that she knows how we operate. She'll have defenses planned, which is why Isabella is going to be our blocker. Sorry, Iz."

Isabella shrugged. She was a muscular woman with dark skin and braided hair. "Happy to take the bullet. Or sword, or fire, or acid. Whatever. S'long as it don't go in my eyes."

Cora unhooked a pair of goggles from her belt and passed them over. Isabella nodded her thanks as she took them.

"Dorothy won't go quietly, or easily. We'll have a fight on our hands." She nodded at Alma. "That's where you come in. While we're distracting her, you take Florence through the wall into the vault next door to the townhouse. That place is locked up tight, so she won't anticipate an attack from that flank. Once you get in, you'll go up to the second floor. You'll send a Florence in, two if you're feeling up to it, and attack her from behind."

Violet raised her hand. "When you say 'attack,' just how violent will this encounter be?"

"That's entirely up to Dorothy," Trafalgar said. "She was quick to anger during our visit earlier, so I have no doubt she'll defend herself. I honestly don't know where she'll draw the line. It will be our goal not to harm her, but we have to be prepared to defend ourselves."

Violet looked disturbed by that, but she nodded.

"If anyone has doubts about our plan, it's best to bring them up now. Convince me there's another way."

"No," Violet said. "I don't know Dorothy Boone as well as the rest of you, but I know her well enough. If she's determined, she will not back down quietly. We have to do everything in our power to make her see the light. Hopefully once she's herself again, she'll thank us for doing what was necessary."

Trafalgar nodded. "We can only hope."

After one final check to make sure everyone else was in agreement before heading out. Violet stayed behind but gave Trafalgar a long kiss of good luck before letting her leave. She confirmed Dorothy was still at home and told them to be careful.

They drove to Threadneedle and stopped a block away to let Florence and Alma get out so they could approach unseen. Trafalgar parked in front of the house, the same space she had taken earlier, and let Isabella lead the way up the stairs. Zilla glanced at Trafalgar and tried to read her expression.

"Everything okay, Mrs. Rhys?"

"Just trying to be content with hiding behind someone so they'll get hurt instead of me."

Isabella looked over her shoulder and smiled. She had fitted the goggles over her eyes but her wink was still easy to see.

"Don't worry, Trav. Been a long time since anything's hurt me too bad. Anything comes out of that doorway, I'd much rather it hit me than one of you."

Trafalgar smiled and patted the larger woman on the arm. "I'll try to let that comfort me, Iz. Thank you."

She waited long enough to give the other part of their team a chance to get into position, then said, "Okay," and stepped back. Isabella knocked on the door and stood up straight. Her torso seemed to expand a bit to cover both Trafalgar and Zilla. Trafalgar waited, fighting the urge to elbow Isabella out of the way so she could face Dorothy properly. Her hands were itching, and she was very aware of how many weapons she had hidden on her.

Thirty seconds passed, and then two minutes. Isabella looked back at Trafalgar.

"Try again."

Isabella knocked harder. "Lady Boone! We need to have a conversation. Miss Trafalgar is here."

They waited. Trafalgar lowered her head and closed her eyes.

She'd known as soon as she drew the damn map that Dorothy would throw a wrench into the plan. She didn't expect it to happen quite this early, had expected to at least get in the door, but it was starting to look like they would be forced to improvise the whole damn thing. Either that or find some way to signal Florence and Alma that the plan was canceled and come back another time.

"I've said everything I need to say to Trafalgar."

She looked up, Dorothy's voice muffled by the door but still loud and clear. "Dorothy, please."

"The bulletproof brawler and the Knock-Out Dame?" Dorothy said. "Are you really that scared of me? Am I really *that* alarming?"

"Your actions have been erratic," Trafalgar called back. "Surely you have to see that. And if you can't, then it's just more evidence that you need help. We're talking about time travel here, Dorothy! If you really can travel back as far as you want, a few days won't make any difference. Just to be absolutely certain that you're doing the right thing before you take actions that can't be taken back."

"I've already waited seven years to have Beatrice back," Dorothy said, the anguish clear in her voice despite the door between them. "I shouldn't have to wait longer. She shouldn't have to live this non-existence a second longer than necessary!"

"I agree," Trafalgar said. "If Beatrice does still exist somewhere, I will be absolutely horrified to think of what she's been through over these past few years. But even so, I have no doubt she would also argue against acting rashly."

Dorothy said, "There is nothing rash about my actions, Trafalgar. And I do have to say, it's a laugh to hear you preach about not rushing into a plan when you're doing the exact same thing."

Trafalgar tensed. "I'm not sure—"

"I knew the tools you had at your disposal, Trafalgar. The Society apprentices and all their varied powers. I may not have spent much time working with them, but I've kept tabs on everyone. I know who has maintained their powers, and I know who is available. And I know what tactics you're most likely to employ. Distraction. Check. Flank attack. Check."

Trafalgar looked toward the vault. "Dorothy, what have you done?"

"Only defended myself," Dorothy said. "Alma Jessup, the ability to pass through walls, like the walls of my vault. And she can't bring many people to back her up, but she can bring one person with the ability to become a half dozen. I've had a lot of time, Trafalgar. My mind was a bit jumbled when we spoke earlier, but it's only gotten clearer. Six years before I went back. And I didn't spend every single moment focused on a single problem. No. No, I've taken breaks. I've drawn maps, written articles, and researched the newest members of our group. Better safe than sorry, right? After all, they were all criminals before they signed up with us."

Trafalgar was horribly aware of the fact that she couldn't get inside the vault to help Alma and Florence. "Don't hurt them."

"They aren't hurt. Well... not fatally. I researched a substance that even she was unable to phase through, just in case we were ever faced with detaining her. She encountered that as soon as she entered the foyer of the building next door. She's currently encased in it. She can breathe, she can move around, but walls and floors are as solid to her as they are to everyone else."

Trafalgar was breathing hard. Zilla and Isabella were both looking at her, desperate for some kind of signal for what they should do.

"And Florence?"

Dorothy clucked her tongue. "Now she might suffer a little, I'm afraid. It's amazing what can trigger her to duplicate. Kinetic force, like slapping or pinching herself, but I discovered that a certain frequency of sonic vibration will cause it. Inaudible to the human ear, but unmistakable to whatever is happening in her cells when she splits. The noise is triggered by weight sensors in the floor. As long as she's standing on it, the sound will continue, and she will duplicate, and duplicate, and duplicate, until she simply passes out from the strain. Nothing fatal, as I said, but it will take her a few days to recover."

Trafalgar pushed Isabella out of the way. "You truly have gone mad!" she shouted at the door. "Stop this at once! Those women--"

Dorothy shouted back with equal rage. "*Those women* came to *my home* to assault me! This was once your home as well, *Mrs. Rhys*, and I'm positive you remember the lengths I will go to in order to defend it. Besides, it was all merely hypothetical. Alma and Florence are perfectly fine. I only said that to get you in front of your shield."

"You--"

The front door exploded outward in a flash of light, smoke, and splinters. Trafalgar was thrown backward into Isabella, who tried to catch her but was also bowled backward down the stairs by the force of the blast. The two of them tumbled into Zilla, and all three landed in a heap on the pavement. Isabella came down hard on Zilla, who let out a frighteningly wet and choked sound as the air was crushed from her chest.

Dorothy emerged from the house in a mask that covered her eyes and mouth, protecting her from the smoke. She wore a long purple coat, buttoned to the collar, and held the weapon she'd used to blow open the door in one hand. Its flared barrel was pointed at the sky, which was rapidly turning dark purple with night. Dorothy stood over the sprawled bodies of the woman and cocked her head to the side.

"I don't doubt you could have done a better job if you had more time to plan. But this is me warning you against trying again. I don't want to hurt you. I don't want to hurt any of the women we've taken into our charge. But I will not allow you to hinder my mission. This is the only mission I've ever had that matters. This is what my life has been building to."

Trafalgar pushed herself up on her elbows. "Beatrice is dead, Dorothy. She's gone. I'm sorry. I'm so sorry, and I've done everything in my power to not say those words, but you need to hear them. She's gone."

Dorothy lowered the gun and aimed it at Trafalgar's face. Trafalgar didn't flinch.

"Will you kill me, Dorothy? Will that be part of your triumphant tale of rescuing the lost maiden? Shooting your friend, your ally, your lover, in the face? Will Beatrice look at you with awe and admiration when she hears of how you killed me in the street like a dog?"

Dorothy huffed. A moment later, she lowered the gun.

"Do not follow me, Trafalgar. This is your warning."

She turned with a sweep of her coat and stalked away down the street, never once looking back.

"She'll be fine."

Dorothy muttered this under her breath, her voice muffled by the mask she wore. Everyone on the street was quick to step out of her way. She knew it was only a matter of time before someone called the police, if not for the exploding door then for the suspicious person walking near the banks in a mask, so she pulled off the mask to make herself look a little less conspicuous. Her hair stood up in spikes and her arm, weighed down by the gun, swung like a dead piece of wood at her side.

"She's fine," she said again. She swiped her hand over her face, clearing it of sweat and feeling just how hot her cheeks and forehead had become.

Trafalgar had been conscious when Dorothy left her. Confused, perhaps concussed, but in one piece. The gun was a weapon of terror, not destruction. It only blew the door apart because the barrel had been pressed tightly against it when she pulled the trigger. She wouldn't have done it if she thought they would actually be hurt...

Although the woman on the bottom of the pile had looked extremely pained when Dorothy left...

No. She couldn't think about that. Broken eggs and omelets and all that. If everything went according to plan, and there was no reason for her to believe it wouldn't, these days would be overwritten by another version of reality. A better version. She and Trafalgar had once died in a South American cave only to awaken in a new world. They survived, they lived on. Beatrice could live on as well. She just had to have the courage to see it through to the end.

She couldn't do it alone, and Trafalgar wasn't the only one with access to magical Londoners. If she'd had more time, she could have contacted Cecil and used him as a secret weapon, but she couldn't risk playing that card with Trafalgar on her doorstep. Luckily he wasn't the only ace she had up her sleeve. In seeking out information about the new members of the Mnemosyne Society, she'd found dozens of other people who had gained powers in recent years but kept a low profile about it. She maintained a record of every person she confirmed along with their ability, just in case the time came when she needed a little magical help.

That time had arrived.

The problem was that any lead she got on those sources would be immediately compromised by Trafalgar's wife. Damned unfair to be running from someone who could pinpoint your location anywhere in the world just by closing her damned eyes.

Dorothy knew she had a solid head start; Trafalgar wouldn't leave her allies trapped in the vault suffering at the hands of her trap. She did feel guilty about that, but not terribly so. The traps would only have been sprung if someone entered without permission, and they were designed to target only very specific individuals. She was only defending her property from intruders. Anything that happened to them was their own fault.

She traveled west toward St. Paul's, to one of the narrow streets shooting off from Ludgate Hill, to a tiny sliver of a storefront only wide enough for a glass door next to a four-square window pasted over with faded sales announcements. The door was papered over but a sliver of light was visible around the edges, so she let herself inside and pulled the door shut behind her.

The interior of the restaurant was smaller than almost every parlor she'd ever seen. There was one table with two chairs. A counter at the far end of the room blocked off the kitchen, which was the source of the thick humid air that filled the cursed box. A man behind the counter was reading a paperback novel and didn't stop reading when she entered. She knew from their last encounter that he was of average height but below average weight. His shirt seemed to swim on his skeletal arms and torso, and the skin of his face looked painted onto the bone.

"What can I get for you, love?" he muttered without moving his lips.

"Distance," she said. "Is your wife in?"

He finally looked up, snorted, and went back to his book. "You."

Dorothy approached the counter. "Yes. Me. I'm afraid I must insist. It's quite urgent, and something of an emergency."

He turned a page. "Said last time you'd leave us alone."

"Yes, I said that I wouldn't bother you unless it was necessary. I'm afraid–"

"She doesn't want anything to do with you."

Dorothy rolled her eyes and reached across the counter. She snatched the book from him, tossed it aside, and grabbed a handful of his collar. He locked both hands around her wrist, inadvertently helping her pull him across the counter. He fell to the floor at her feet and she let him see the barrel of her weapon before he even tried getting back up. For the first time since she'd come into the restaurant, she had his full attention. Despite that, the answer came from behind the counter.

"Yes, his wife is here. And she will thank you not to bang him up too much."

Dorothy looked over her shoulder. Nathalie Huston's dark, annoyed gaze was fixed on her, although she was positive the irritation was due to Dorothy breaking her promise than what she'd done to Ronald. She was wearing a high-necked chef tunic and her brown hair was bundled under a toque. She pointed at the floor and then jerked her thumb up. Dorothy took the hint and allowed Ronald to get to his feet.

"You're not welcome here, Lady Boone." Ronald went around the counter to safety, and Nathalie brushed off his shirt as she continued speaking. "Thought we made that clear last time."

"Things have changed."

"I can see that." She looked at the shaggy mess Dorothy had made of her hair. "Let me make it easy for you. Whatever you've got running, whatever danger you have on your heels, we're not interested. We're doing just fine without sticking our noses where they don't belong."

"People are going to come looking for me sooner rather than later. If they find me here, your noses will be deep in it whether they belong or not. You can make sure they find me elsewhere."

Nathalie twisted her lips and banged her fist on the counter as if keeping a beat, then growled loudly as she motioned Dorothy around the counter.

"Damn it, Boone, come on. But this is the last time you darken my door."

"That is a promise I will have no trouble keeping."

They went into the kitchen, leaving Ronald behind. Nathalie looked back at her.

"So where exactly are you going?"

"Just north of Paris. Nanterre."

Nathalie stopped next to the storeroom. "I hope you have a way home, because you're not getting back this way."

"You let me worry about that."

Nathalie rested her hands on the door and bowed her head. She closed her eyes, hunched her shoulders, and swept her palms down the metal. Dorothy could have sworn she felt the kitchen tiles under her feet shudder. Nathalie let out a breath and slumped forward, catching herself before she could fall. She pressed the back of her hand against her forehead and tugged the door handle up. When she opened it, Dorothy was presented with the sight of a dark alley that couldn't possibly extend from the back of the restaurant as it backed up against another building.

"Nanterre awaits," Nathalie said. "*Allons-y.*"

Nathalie's power was to open doors, connecting one part of the planet with another, no matter how distant. She'd never explained what it took out of her, but judging by the pallor of her skin and the beads of sweat dotting her forehead and upper lip, it was a lot.

"Thank you," Dorothy said as she moved to step through. "For what it's worth, I guarantee I won't bother you again."

Nathalie gripped Dorothy's arm in a tight, painful grip. "If you do," Nathalie said quietly, "I will not send you where you ask. I can open doors anywhere, Lady Boone, and if you insist on bringing your madness to me, putting my life and that of my husband at risk, I will not hesitate to open one in a very dark place and drag you through. Am I understood?"

Dorothy held eye contact for five seconds before she nodded. "You have my word."

Nathalie let her go and stepped back, one hand on the door in anticipation of slamming it shut. Dorothy stepped over the threshold and turned in time to see the metal storeroom door swing back into place, cutting off the London kitchen she'd just left. For a moment there was the shape of it in the air, and then it dissipated like a static charge. All that remained was a solid brick wall with a rusted water pipe running up its length.

This part of the plan would have been immensely easier with Trafalgar's wife and her ability. Dorothy had been forced to rely on public records, and even those could be years out of date. She had a public registry which told her where the man she sought had lived in 1919, and she could only pray he'd never moved.

It took her some time to determine where Nathalie's doorway had delivered her. Once she had that information, she followed a map of the commune to a block of apartment buildings in the center of town. The courtyard in the center of the cluster was home to a playground that had seen better days and an empty swimming pool. It was twilight, with the sun too low in the sky to see, but she had a feeling the swing set and climbing frame made of painted metal pipes would have been abandoned even at mid-day.

Dorothy climbed the stairs to the third story, found the door marked with the numbers from the registry, and knocked. She held her breath, eyes closed, praying for a miracle.

"*Oui?*" from the other side of the door.

Dorothy snapped her head up. She responded in French as well. "Good afternoon, yes, my name is Dorothy Boone. I am hoping to speak to Mr. Henri Durocher."

Silence from the other side of the door. "He's dead."

She tried to push down the despair those words caused. "Ah, if that were truly the case, there would have been no need for hesitation. So either you are lying and *you* are Mr. Durocher, or he is there and you had to consult with him before you replied. Either way, I only wish to speak with him about–"

"The past," he interrupted. "Old and forgotten times."

"Old, yes," Dorothy said. "Forgotten... no. Definitely not."

More silence. Dorothy stepped back from the door and looked both ways down the corridor. She was about to speak again, completely clueless about what her next tactic would be, when the door opened. The man who stood before her was in his late fifties but looked capable of taking on someone half his age. His black hair had receded into a widows peak, but his beard was a full and solid white. His cheeks were sunken, as were the green eyes that he fixed on her. He kept one hand on the door as if he intended to slam it shut at any second.

"Dorothy Boone. Lady Dorothy Boone?"

"That's right."

"I've heard of you." He pressed his lips together. His grip on the door seemed to relax somewhat. "You're not the first to come looking for me."

"I would be shocked if I was. Honestly, I only want to talk. I need to know what happened back then."

"Just talk?"

"A conversation. Maybe a few questions, but at the end of it, I walk away and you never see me again."

Durocher looked away from her as he considered the offer. Finally he pushed the door open wider and swept his arm to indicate she should enter.

"I will give you one hour, Lady Boone, based on your reputation. Please, step inside, and I will tell you how I unleashed magic on this world and doomed us all."

CHAPTER FOUR

THE DAMAGE report wasn't as devastating as it could have been, but Trafalgar felt the suffering of her friends was entirely her fault.

Zilla had five broken ribs from Isabella falling on her. The woman could barely breathe, and had to be rushed to the hospital for emergency care. Trafalgar hadn't even go with her because she and Isabella had to get into the townhouse and break their way into the vault to save Alma and Florence from the trap Dorothy had set. Alma could still maneuver in the bizarre, gelatinous netting Dorothy had caught her in, so she was waiting by the door trying to get the lock open when Trafalgar broke it down.

"I can get myself out of this mess," Alma said. "But Flo... Trafalgar, she's... she's..."

"I know. We'll take care of her."

To Trafalgar's horror, Dorothy hadn't been bluffing. She counted eighteen Florences, and four more appeared by the time she determined which one was the original. She was lying on the floor, eyes rolled back in her head and heels clicking out a desperate SOS on the floorboards as she summoned yet another duplicate of herself. The new arrival looked around for a moment, confused, then collapsed and joined the others in the seizing pile of women on the floor.

There was only one way for someone else to make one of

Florence's dupes reabsorb to the whole. So while she was sicked by the idea, Trafalgar cradled Florence's head to her chest and nodded for Isabella to do the unthinkable. Isabella grimaced, chose one of the duplicates at random, and murdered it as efficiently as possible by snapping its neck.

She worked as quickly as she could, but the Florences kept coming. Trafalgar tried not to hear the sound as each one was dispatched, which made her think of the trigger. Sound. As long as Florence was in this room, she would keep creating more and more. She wiped her eyes and picked up Florence's limp but shivering body and carried her to the stairs.

"Don't stop," she shouted without looking back. "They must all be eliminated before she can even begin to heal!"

"Doing what I can!"

She took Florence to the top floor of Dorothy's townhouse, as far from the vault lobby as possible, and laid her on Dorothy's bed. The seizing had slowed down, and her color was a little better. Her eyes were closed now, which gave her hope that the poor woman was getting a respite from whatever horrors she'd been through.

All told, it took Isabella twenty minutes to kill thirty-two Florences. When she came out to tell Trafalgar the deed was done, her face was completely devoid of color and her hands were shaking. She walked to the bed and lightly touched Florence's cheek, then her lips, as if checking to make sure she was real and breathing.

"I might need to take some time... away," Isabella whispered.

Trafalgar remembered the strong woman's brave words down on the street, how it had been a long time since anything had hurt her too badly. She had a feeling she wouldn't be making that boast anymore.

"As long as you need, my friend. But I assure you, Florence will thank you for what you did tonight. You saved her."

"Don't know if I'm ready to hear all that, truth be told. But thank you. F-for trying."

Trafalgar nodded. Isabella turned and left the room, her heavy footsteps thudding down the steps to the front of the house. Trafalgar tried not to think about how familiar, and yet how utterly alien this room seemed. She rubbed her hands together and, in doing so, realized they were caked with something. She looked down with a frown. Her palms were gray, gritty, and the same substance was on her trousers and smeared across one of her sleeves.

"What in the world...?"

Dust. She was covered in dust. Once she had identified it, she looked around the bedroom. Every surface had a fine layer of dust on it. The dresser, the bedposts, even the floor revealed the ghostly shape of footprints from those who had been passing back and forth recently.

If Dorothy had been living here as a shut-in for the past year, there should not have been this much dust. Not in a heavily trafficked area, certainly not in her bedroom.

But if she hadn't been in the house...

Her train of thought was interrupted by the sound of footsteps on the stairs, which soon resolved into Alma Jessup standing in the doorway.

"She... she doing okay?"

"I don't know yet," Trafalgar said. She was very aware that she'd once sat vigil next to Beatrice Sek in this very bed, the same position. She closed her eyes and pressed her thumb against the bridge of her nose. "We sacrifice so much for this ridiculous profession. What's it all for. Knowledge? Some knickknacks that we keep locked away out of sight because they're too dangerous? Letting beautiful and remarkable people get hurt and die for a footnote in a history book."

Alma came into the room. "We're doing it so people won't be forgotten. So lessons won't be forgotten. People have always been people, and we're bound to make the same mistakes. So if we know what happened before, we can stop ourselves from going through it all again. Knowing the past makes us smarter, stronger, more likely to survive. That's an important cause."

"One worth dying for?"

"Sure," Alma said with a sad chuckle. "Never really understood that whole thing, you know? Worth dying for. People die for things every day. People die because there's a gas leak in their house. They die because they happened to be too close to someone who wanted money. Man got trampled by a horse just this past week. Didn't do nothing to it, might never have seen a horse before that day, but he still died for the horse in a way.

"I don't think anything's worth dying for, Miss Trafalgar. But I think if you're doing something worthwhile when your time comes, that takes a little of the sting out of it. I know if that netting shit had cut off my oxygen and everything went black, I wouldn't have been wishing I was still out on the street getting a knife in my gut for whatever silver I had in my pocket."

Trafalgar's eyes had closed during Alma's speech. "Thank you, Alma. That is something I've needed to hear for a very long time. I believe I agree with you completely."

"Good. Glad I could help." She stood and walked to Trafalgar, bending down to awkwardly hug her. "After I got the stuff off, I called your office. Violet is on her way."

"Ah, fantastic. I was worried I would be the only one who didn't suffer some kind of torture tonight."

Alma said, "I'll head out when she arrives."

"Thank you, Alma, but I'll go down to greet her. If you wouldn't mind sitting with Florence until she awakens."

"It'd be my honor."

Trafalgar stood up and Alma took her seat. Trafalgar left and descended the stairs, almost to the foyer before Violet appeared in the shattered doorway. Violet scanned the damage, then swept her eyes up to her wife standing above her on the stairs.

"Now... my love, if you'll let me explain..."

Violet started up the stairs. "Are you hurt?"

"No. I'm~"

Violet cut her off with a kiss. Trafalgar didn't question it; she wrapped her arms around her wife and returned the kiss with passion.

"I'm angry with you," Violet said when they parted.

Trafalgar cupped Violet's cheek. "I can tell."

Violet turned her head to kiss Trafalgar's palm. "I'm too relieved that you're okay to show it right now. But the anger is coming."

"I consider myself duly warned."

Violet stroked her hands over the shoulders of Trafalgar's blouse as she examined the scene around them.

"Do we know yet if everyone will be okay?"

"Too early to say for certain. Alma and Isabella both seem relatively unharmed from the experience, so they're tending to the injured. I need to know where Dorothy is."

Violet said, "I assumed, so I found her on the way over. But it doesn't make sense. She's just outside Paris."

"What?" Trafalgar shook her head. "That's impossible. She left here less than an hour ago."

"I've checked multiple times. There's no sign of her anywhere in England so it can't be a duplicate reading."

Trafalgar knew those were possible; they had once spent a week tracking a stolen necklace which had been broken up into its component parts and spread all across the country. She hadn't suspected Dorothy was somehow split into pieces and scattered across the globe, but she couldn't think of a way she might have gotten to an entirely different country in the time since they'd last seen each other.

"It's a mystery we'll have to solve later," she said with some reluctance. She stepped out of Violet's embrace and headed upstairs. "If she really is in Paris, there's no way we can follow her. Hopefully she's left something here that can help us catch up with her."

Violet followed her. "Do you think there's still a chance to stop her?"

"She implied she could time travel without leaving this house. At least the impression I got was that she hadn't come back to the townhouse following her alleged adventure in 1910. If she had been outside, she would have noticed the new building at the end of the street and known time had passed. So she wouldn't need to leave to complete her plan. Let alone travel all the way to Paris. There's something she needs before she can go back."

Trafalgar was behind Dorothy's desk now, examining the debris littering its surface. Papers, some of which had been wadded up and then smoothed out, open books stacked on top of other open books, pages that had been torn out with notes scrawled in the margins. She also saw half-finished maps and knew they were what Dorothy worked on when she wanted to distract her brain while it worked on a complicated problem.

"Do you need me to keep tabs on her?" Violet asked.

"If you're able. I need to know if she suddenly reappears in London or takes a detour to New York." She furrowed her brow. "We don't know anyone who can teleport, do we? None of the apprentices have mentioned that ability?"

"Not that I've heard. But we haven't even scratched the surface of every talent in London."

Trafalgar sighed. "I doubt we will ever have a full accounting. Shame." She found a list of names and moved it toward the window, but the fading light was too dim to see. "Could you…" The overhead light came on, and Trafalgar smiled at Violet. "Thank you, love."

"Anything interesting?"

"Names," Trafalgar said, "but none I recognize. But look here, top of the list." She turned the paper so Violet could see. "Henri Durocher. No one I've ever heard of, but it certainly sounds French to me. Can you tell me anything?"

Violet closed her eyes and immediately flinched away. "There are too many people with that name. I can't even get a vague impression of any specific one. We need more details."

Trafalgar said, "Can you focus on France?"

"Not without more to go on. Even knowing the general area Dorothy's in doesn't help me. I'm sorry."

"No, no, I'm sorry. I know how your abilities work. I was just hoping for a miracle."

Violet held out her hand for the paper. "Let me see the whole list. Maybe a combination of names will trigger something when I combine it with France."

"Brilliant." Trafalgar handed it over and sat down in Dorothy's chair to continue the search of her desk. The drawers were locked, of course.

"Pencil jar," Violet said without looking up from the paper.

Trafalgar upended the jar into the already messy desk, then fished around in the bottom until she found the key. She smiled and held it up for Violet to see.

"You really *are* a miracle, my love."

Violet smiled but kept reading.

Trafalgar unlocked the top left drawer and began cataloguing what she found there. Her mind continued rolling around the elements she knew of Dorothy's plan.

"1910 is a peculiar year. The War didn't begin until 1914, and it was some time before magic was used for combat. Why would she plan to arrive so early?"

"Perhaps she needs time to set things into motion. And we all know tensions were building long before war was officially declared. The Balkan conflicts..."

"Yes, but one woman can't possibly hope to prevent something so massive, even if that woman is Lady Dorothy Boone. There has to be something else guiding her movements." She tapped her finger on the edge of the desk. "She doesn't intend to stop the War, because she knows it's inevitable. Too many powerful countries with feelings that have been too hurt for too long. She would have to go back fifty... a hundred... hell, she'd probably have to start centuries ago to ensure the conflict never happened at all. She isn't foolish enough to try."

"Therefore...?" Violet prompted.

"She's not trying to stop the War. She can only stop the use of magic to fight it."

Violet looked up. "Can she do that?"

"I don't know. Possibly." Trafalgar started examining the books open on the desktop, reading the title of each one before she discarded it for the one below or next to it. She finally found what she was looking for and held it up so Violet could read the title.

"Magick and Its Use On the Front Lines."

Trafalgar nodded and began to flip through the pages. "I should have recognized the name when I saw it. Maybe I hit my head when I fell outside. Blast." She found a page near the beginning. "The other names on the list... one of them is Theodore Wysocki."

"Yes. I was able to locate him in South Korea."

"Francis William Turnbull."

Violet nodded. "Yes. Who are they?"

"According to this book, they're three of the five men who brought magic to the War. Without their interference, it likely would never have been introduced as a weapon. That's the only thing Dorothy has to stop. The rest of the War can happen as long as it's only fought with mundane weapons."

"So if these men are responsible for everything..."

"Then I believe Dorothy intends to ask these men directly where they were before the War started."

"Then she just has to go back and~"

"Hunt them," Trafalgar said. "They have no reason not to tell her where they were twenty years ago, so they'll be forthcoming with the information. Once she has it, nothing will be stopping her from going back and hunting them down, one by one."

"Nothing but us," Violet corrected.

Trafalgar pressed her lips together rather than confirming what she'd just said. They had no choice. Dorothy had to be stopped, and no one else was capable of getting close enough to do it. And if Dorothy believed this was the only way to save Beatrice, she would not be easily stopped. She had to prepare herself for the possibility that it would come down to killing Dorothy to save the world.

She hoped she would be able to make the right decision when that time came.

Henri turned on a lamp as he passed the divan into the kitchen, casting a weak glow over the cavern of his living space. Dorothy stood just across the threshold and took in the sight. It was a small apartment and it seemed as if he was living exclusively in a single room. Stacks of books and newspapers formed a barrier between the divan and his bed, which was shrouded by a curtain of hanging laundry. She also spotted a radio on the floor next to a telephone which seemed to be wrapped in its own cord. The windows were completely covered by blackout curtains that made the room seem more claustrophobic.

He returned with a tin mug which he held out to Dorothy. "It's clean, don't worry. Despite..." He gestured at the disarray. "It's much more organized than it seems."

Dorothy took the mug. "I'm no stranger to orchestrated chaos. Thank you, Monsieur Durocher."

"Henri." He took a seat on the divan. "May I call you Dorothy?"

"Of course." She sat in the armchair facing him. "Regarding your statement at the door, I didn't come here with the intention of blaming you for anything~"

"Oh, you'd be quite correct in doing so," Henri interrupted. "Besides, I know you won't tell the newspapers or write a book. Your opinion is yours alone, and that's the only reason I've agreed to speak with you."

He sipped his drink and stared down at the books on the floor. Dorothy took a sip as well, very weak tea, and waited.

Finally, he began to speak. "I began practicing magic when I was a child. I didn't even know what it was. I didn't know it was unusual. I could move things with my mind, manipulate the world to the way I wanted. Levitation, although not very high. Childish things. I assumed all my friends were doing it as well, but since I never saw it, I thought it was a private thing. So I kept it to myself. It wasn't until I was, mm, a teenager before I understood. By then I was doing bigger things. Manifestations. Teleportation. I admit I didn't always use it for moral reasons, but I was a teenager. I honed my skills but never really thought they would be of much use beyond keeping my purse full, getting free meals, that sort of thing."

"And then the War."

He made a soft noise in his throat. She thought she saw him flinch slightly as he took another sip. "And then the War," he repeated. "A few years before it was actually declared, actually. I think the others and I first met up in 1910, 1911, somewhere in there. We could all sense something big was coming. Some massive change in the air. I thought about signing up for the military, fighting like a regular person. But I kept thinking that if I had these abilities, if I was able to somehow turn the tide, then I owed it to... to the world, to humanity. So I started researching to find out if I really did have the ability to make a difference like that.

"I found others like me. They were doing the same thing. Testing the waters, trying to figure out their powers before they made promises they couldn't keep. Theo. Francis. Angus and GD. We started training together. Learning how to manipulate energy in a way that would be useful to a military. We discovered we were quite good at it, both offensive and defensive magic. We thought we could save lives on both sides, throw water on the fires of war, and bring sense back to the world. Instead we learned that if you offer a sword and a shield, soldiers will take the sword every time."

Dorothy raised an eyebrow and gave him a moment with his thoughts before she pressed on. "You trained here? In Paris?"

Henri nodded. "Angus was staying in a place that had a basement. Abandoned, large and open, plenty of space for experimenting."

"Where, precisely?" Dorothy asked, hoping she wasn't giving away too much of her eagerness. Finding out where Angus Murray was staying in 1910 would be easy enough with access to public records, but she was hoping to hit the ground running as soon as she went back.

"What does that matter?"

She shook her head. "It doesn't really, I suppose. I'm just trying to envision it."

He swirled his cup again, already lost in his own mind. "I barely remember the details anyway. Somewhere in the nineteenth arrondissement. It didn't take us long before we decided we were ready. We stayed in touch. Practiced. Got stronger in our abilities. When war was finally declared, we met up again and made a vow to do everything in our power to be the men who saved the world. It wasn't about country, it wasn't about winning, necessarily. We thought if we offered our services to as many sides as possible, no one would dare risk confrontation."

Dorothy could see the guilt on his face, so she refrained from pointing out how stupid this idea was. As he'd said, offer a sword and a shield...

"We split up and went to our respective leaders to tell them what we could do. At that point, as far as I know, we were the only adept practitioners of magic in the entire world. I manipulated an audience with Prime Minister Viviani and showed him what I could do. He took my offer to President Poincaré, and he enlisted me on the spot. He wanted me to begin training soldiers immediately. 'Strictly defensive measures,' he said. 'Keep our men safe and alive.' I warned him that not everyone would be able to practice magic. He assured me he would take whatever I could produce. We created so many practitioners in those first months. So many..."

He stared off into the distance again, the mug hovering near his lips for a long minute before he finally took a sip.

"To this day, I don't know if there was an official order to change tactics. There's a chance that Poincaré secretly demanded his soldiers start learning how to hurt the enemy, or if the soldiers took the initiative on their own. It might have been both, who knows. It doesn't matter in the end. The only thing of consequence is that the tide shifted. Soon I was watching men train with fireballs, energy attacks, binding spells. Shields turned into barriers and quickly became prisons. I didn't know how to stop what I'd started. Hell, I didn't know if I had a right to stop them. This was *the War*, the one to end all wars, the fate of civilization hanging in the balance. If I had snuffed out magic and then we went on to lose, I would never be able to live with it on my conscience. So I let it happen."

Dorothy said, "And the right people won. So perhaps you did the right thing."

Henri snorted and looked at her. "You of all people know better than that, Lady Boone. I read the newspapers." He kicked the stack next to his foot. "You've fought the beasts our meddling woke. You stopped the devastating plague that could have wiped out the entire world. We lit a match and dropped it in a pool of gas. You and Trafalgar Rhys have done everything in your power to snuff it out, but the spark is still there and the room is filling with fumes. Soon something will awaken that no one will be able to hold back, and this glorious world we know will crumble just like all the ones that came before it."

"I don't think that's possible," Dorothy said, feigning confidence. "I believe we're stronger, more resilient, and we can withstand any curses that might come our way. Magic or mundane."

He shook his head, smiling sadly. "Do you know the five extinctions, Lady Boone?"

"Yes. And please, call me Dorothy."

He stood and went back to the kitchen, talking as he refilled his mug. "The first time, volcanoes wiped out all life on Earth. The second time, it was likely global cooling. The third was called the Great Dying and the planet took thirty million years to recover from the losses. The fourth was likely a combination of factors... climate change, asteroid impacts..." He came back and sank into his seat again with a sigh. "And then the latest. The one everyone thinks about when they think about mass extinctions. An asteroid colliding with the Earth and wiping out the dinosaurs. The big one. Sixty-six million years ago. All of these events changed the world, made it unrecognizable, but there's one other thing they all have in common."

Dorothy said, "And what might that be, Mr. Durocher?"

"None of them were caused by the species that were wiped out. If this is the sixth massive extinction in Earth's history, we have no one to blame but ourselves."

He looked into his newly-full cup, grimaced, and set it aside. He folded his hands and looked up at her, holding eye contact.

"Tell me something, Lady Boone. You're not here on some esoteric fact-finding mission. You've been largely absent since the events in London seven years ago. You've been working on something massive. You don't have to tell me what it is. Just tell me one thing... can you fix the mistakes I made?"

Dorothy held his gaze. "I believe I can."

"Then do whatever is necessary. Promise me you'll stop at nothing."

Dorothy pressed her lips together. "Even if things end much differently for you? Even if it means your death?"

Henri laughed and sagged against the back of his chair. "Look at how I live. Guilt devours me. Every day brings a new terror. Killing me would be a mercy, and even if I don't know the good my death will bring, in my heart I will know it's a righteous end." He leaned forward, his eyes burning into hers. "Promise me, Dorothy."

She reached out and took his hand. "You have my word, Henri. Whatever it takes."

CHAPTER FIVE

VIOLET CONFIRMED that Denys and Turnbull from Dorothy's potential hit list were deceased. The other two men Angus Murray and Gerard "GD" Denys. Neither name rang any bells for Trafalgar, but the names were just unusual enough for her to be sure they were the right men. Trafalgar flipped through the book and skimmed as much as she could about the men. She knew some of it, information gleaned from years of history lessons and half-heard ruminations by Dorothy and other scholars on the subject, but she'd never been particularly interested in the specifics of the War.

Violet said, "How did five men give magic to entire armies?"

"I said one woman couldn't affect the entire War, but it was in fact spurred along by a relatively small group of men across Europe. Presidents and Prime Ministers and war councils... a handful of men sitting in rooms and making decisions that affected millions of people. Durocher, Wysocki, and the others approached their respective leaders and made them an offer. A weapon. By offering it to multiple powers, they hoped to inspire peace."

"You can destroy us, but we can destroy you in return, so why don't we both just agree not to fight."

"Exactly. Unfortunately when countries began joining forces, the threat of mutually assured destruction wasn't such a deterrent anymore. They were afraid of the enemy discovering what they had, or learning to wield it themselves, so the best defense was to strike first while they had the element of surprise." She paged through a book until she found a Chapter, handing it over to Violet. "The third of October in Arleux, France. The Battle of Arras. The first recorded use of magic in the war. A French practitioner made three German battalions vanish in a flash of light. They were later discovered to have been transported off the battlefield to an island in the Mediterranean.

"Word spread. Soon enough the Germans were experimenting with their own magicians, and magic became just another weapon in the arsenal."

"I never knew about any of this," Violet said. "I was a teenager and just focused on surviving. By the time I heard about magical soldiers, everyone treated it as just... something that had always been part of the fighting."

Trafalgar said, "That quickly became the case. Practitioners became the elite fighting squadrons, with other infantry tasked with keeping them safe. Anyone performing magic was a high-value target for the enemy, so they had to be protected at all costs. But even with supernatural weapons at play, the War finally came to an end because of very human concerns. One side simply had more soldiers, a seemingly inexhaustible supply, and the enemy couldn't defend their lines any longer. They were cut off from their food and oil and peace was their only chance of survival."

"So even with magic, it was a lost cause."

"Indeed. There are no shortcuts to victory. No matter how powerful your weapon may be, it's meaningless without someone to wield it."

They fell silent and continued examining their books for more evidence. Trafalgar was about to give up on her current book and choose another when Helena Swan appeared in the office doorway. She was an apprentice with the Keepings, one who had lost her magical abilities but was still an extremely talented researcher. She'd arrived earlier with a few other members of the Society, including a doctor who was tending to Florence.

"Excuse me, ma'ams. Isabella said you believed Lady Boone was traveling in time without leaving the townhouse."

"That's the working theory," Trafalgar said. "If she was traveling at all, I can't imagine she left the building."

Helena said, "If that's so, then I believe I found something you'll be interested in."

Trafalgar put down the book and stood. Violet indicated she would stay and continue researching. Helena led Trafalgar up to the upper level of the house, to a door next to Dorothy's bedroom. She opened it and revealed a narrow space Trafalgar hadn't even known existed. It was slanted along the angle of the roof, making it difficult for either of them to stand upright. Helena stopped in the center of the space and crouched, reached down, and brushed two fingers over the wooden floor.

"Something was placed here. Almost but not quite circular. You can see where it heated up on the outside and scarred the planks."

Trafalgar crouched as well. The markings were dim but, once she knew to look for them, unmistakable. Something had definitely been placed in that closet and was then heated up to a high temperature.

"You didn't find anything that could have made these marks?"

"Nothing just lying around," Helena said. "But I imagine if it is some kind of artifact that allows her to travel in time, she wouldn't be too reckless with it."

"And yet, she wasn't carrying anything like this when she left the house earlier. It's a simple conclusion that she concealed it somewhere on the premises." She twisted and looked back into the hallway as if she would see a marked trail leading to wherever the object was hidden. It was the smallest of threads, but at least now they had some idea of how large their trophy might be. Whatever it was, finding it was key. If they could confiscate the item, it didn't matter where Dorothy was in the world or how she'd gotten there. Her plan would be impossible.

"Excellent work, Miss Swan." She stood and brushed off her hands. "Let me know if you notice anything else that might be of interest."

She left the closet and went to the bannister, looking down the stairs. From this vantage point she could see down through the townhouse, all the way to the black-and-white tile of the entry hall. There weren't many places in this house to hide something as big as whatever made the mark in the closet. But Dorothy absolutely knew every single space large enough for the task. Trafalgar had only lived in the house for a few years and knew she hadn't scratched the surface of every nook and cranny. She hadn't even known about that closet, for crying out loud. Who knew how many secret rooms there might be? And that didn't take the vault next door into account, an entire townhouse converted into a safe.

Still, two buildings was a much smaller area of interest than the entire world. Dorothy could jump to Europe - and Trafalgar was still extremely keen to learn how she'd managed that little trick - but this was something they could handle. And maybe Violet could be helpful now that she had a general shape to look for.

Trafalgar went back down to the office and found Violet standing by the desk. "Darling. We're looking for a large circular object approximately the size of-" She was close enough now to see Violet wasn't reading; she was staring at the open book with tears in her eyes. "Violet? What is it? What's wrong?"

Violet placed a trembling finger on the page, which had been filled with Dorothy's horrendous handwriting. Trafalgar turned the book and leaned closer to read the scrawled pencil scratches.

"Unintended consequences of altering/ending/prolonging the War cannot be accurately predicted, however there are certain things which will definitely happen or definitely not happen. One can be certain that the 40 Elephants/Maud Keaton will never gain their abilities. Those women will find themselves trapped once more in meaningless existences, but they arrived there due to their own choices. The fate of the world cannot be ignored for the needs of a handful of foolish women who will, in all likelihood, succumb to their baser instincts given enough time whether they are powered or not."

"It would seem," Violet said, voice trembling, "that your friend did not care much for us."

Trafalgar closed the book and put her hand on Violet's cheek, turning her head until they were looking at each other.

"The Dorothy Boone who wrote those words is an angry, obsessed woman. She is consumed by grief and unable to see past her own pain. She's burning all her bridges... me, the Mnemosyne Society, everyone. She is not herself. She is a shell wearing the face of a woman I once loved, once considered a friend. She is unfeeling. She is cruel. And I will not rest until she is either back in her right mind, or... or secure in a place where she can get help."

Violet took a deep breath and leaned forward, resting her head against Trafalgar's. "I love you, wife."

"Oh, I love you. You and most of the other Elephants led a life of crime because you lacked options. You are a good, honorable woman and nothing will change that. Not Dorothy, not time-travel, not even me." Trafalgar kissed Violet's lips, her hand slipping under Violet's hair to cup the back of her head. "When this matter is settled, you will either have a sincere apology from Dorothy or you will have the satisfaction of living a good, honorable life while she is locked away somewhere she can't hurt anyone."

"You would lock away your friend?"

Trafalgar shook her head. "I would get my friend help, even if that friend fought me tooth and nail. She is clearly in need of help. It's my duty to get it for her." She brushed her thumb across Violet's cheek. "What happens after she's taken into custody will determine our relationship going forward. At this moment she's just a threat. Nothing more."

Violet nodded and stepped back, wiping at her face again. "You, ah... you were going to ask me to find something."

"A ring," Trafalgar said with some reluctance. She felt awkward shifting back to asking favors after reading the drivel Dorothy had written. "It can wait..."

"Jewelry?" Violet said, interrupting her.

"No, larger. Most likely an artifact, approximately one meter in diameter. I believe it's hidden somewhere in this house. Under a floorboard or in a secret compartment–"

Violet was already shaking her head. "No. It's outside. In the backyard, under the shed."

The backyard was so small, so utterly useless, that Trafalgar had entirely forgotten it existed. It was a strip of sod, the grass mostly weathered away to leave patches of exposed cracked dirt. And, in one corner of the space, there was a shack that was always on the verge of falling down. If the backyard was exposed to any kind of strong winds, Trafalgar had no doubt the structure would have collapsed into timber years ago.

She kissed Violet between the eyebrows, then again on the lips. "My brilliant wife strikes again."

"Is it important?"

Trafalgar smiled. "If our theory is correct, then you just completely scuttled Lady Boone's entire plan. It doesn't matter what she's doing in France or who she speaks to when she leaves there. Without the ring, I don't think she can go back in time."

Violet raised her eyebrows. "So we've won."

Trafalgar's smile wavered. "Perhaps for the time being, yes. Come on, let's go retrieve the ring."

She took Violet's hand, leading her out of the room and down the stairs. Finding the ring was a huge victory for them, that was true. But one thing she'd learned from her time working with Dorothy was that one victory, no matter how large, rarely marked the end of the war.

When it came to Dorothy Boone, there were always more battles. She just had to hope they were prepared when she struck.

Dorothy remained with Henri for another hour before she took her leave. He gave her as much information as he could remember, and she filled several pages of her notebook with times, dates, and addresses of the five practitioners' movements before the War. Her hand was shaking when he gripped it in his and gave it a squeeze.

"Your intention may lead to my death," he said, "but I know your success will mean a better world for all of us. I am content with serving that purpose."

"I'll do what I can to ensure your survival," Dorothy promised him. She was quietly thankful that her hands wouldn't be tied. She liked Henri, and during their talk she had been more than a little worried that might affect her when the time came to make a difficult decision. "Before I leave, may I use your telephone? It will be a very long-distance call, but I can leave you some money."

He waved her toward the table. "Call whoever you need. I am beyond caring."

She called an overseas number and, after a brief conversation, thanked Henri for his time and took her leave. She left the building and walked to the rusted playset in the courtyard. She sat down on the swings and pushed her feet against the ground to gently rock back and forth. The chains creaked overhead and she looked up to make sure the crossbar was sturdy enough to hold her weight. Night had completely fallen by that point and the sky was overcast, the clouds illuminated by the glow of red and yellow lights from the town proper.

When she looked down again, a shining crack had appeared in the air directly ahead of her. It was just wide enough for her to see a well-lit parlor on the other side. Dorothy planted her feet and stopped swinging, wrapped her arms around the chains, and watched as two people stepped out of the parlor onto the dying grass of the courtyard. The woman was dressed in riding gear, as if she had just left the stables. Her hair was still up to accommodate a helmet, with a few strands hanging free around her face. The man wore a button-down shirt and slacks but was still as dressed down as Dorothy had ever seen him.

"Why, look who we have here. I hardly recognized you."

"I look downright sloppy," Cecil Dubourne said, plucking at his collar with disdain. "But a few years with the Yanks will do that to you."

It had also greatly diminished his accent. There was still enough to be noticed, but to Dorothy he sounded distinctly American. Cecil and his apprentices were the black sheep of the Mnemosyne Society. They were still officially members in good standing, despite the fact they'd butted heads with the council enough times that he finally announced he was setting off to create a new branch in New York City. It provided enough distance for everyone to remain civil and gave Cecil enough rope that he was able to run his group as he saw fit.

Dorothy had serious suspicions that meant the women still occasionally dabbled in criminal behavior. She couldn't complain since their shady behavior had helped her greatly over the past few years. They helped when she called and, in exchange, she didn't alert the Society of anything she discovered about them.

Including the fact that the woman who just opened the portal between New York and France, Janya Lennox, was one of six women whose powers had actually increased after the purge of magic seven years earlier. Before she had been a cat burglar who could scale walls like a spider and jump from rooftop to rooftop without missing a step. Teleporting was a new ability, as was the silver ring on her left hand.

"Seems as if everyone is pairing up," Dorothy said, nodding at the ring.

Janya smiled proudly. "When you find something worth getting legitimately, you make the effort."

Dorothy forced a smile. She knew, of course, that Janya and Cecil were destined to become a couple. She also knew their eventual child, Riya Lennox, would be born with the ability to travel in time. She was the one who would kick the hornets' nest which had finally ended her partnership with Trafalgar.

"So," Cecil said, looking around for clues. "What are you doing here, Boone?"

"That's none of your concern. I just need Mrs. Lennox's help to get me back to London as expediently as possible."

Cecil and Janya exchanged a look. "About that. Yours wasn't the only call we received this evening. It seems people back home are eager to have you back."

Dorothy tensed. "You didn't tell them where I was, did you? I warn you, Cecil, the things I know about your girls..."

He held up his hands. "No, no. I played the innocent fool. Besides, I couldn't reveal your secret without telling them about Janya's. And I'm sure you have a whole host of blackmail material on my other girls you could unleash if I crossed you."

She raised an eyebrow, acknowledging the fact without confirming it.

"Just know that Trafalgar and Cora are very concerned. I'm supposed to get in contact immediately if you get in touch with us."

"But you won't do that, will you."

He waited a long, tense moment before he finally smiled and shook his head. "No, Dorothy. Of course not. But I want you to remember that I took your side in... whatever this is. The next time I need your help with something, no questions asked."

She sighed. "Fine." It was an easy promise to make. If she succeeded, this conversation would never happen and they'd be living blissfully in another timeline.

"Now that we have that out of the way," Cecil said.

Janya held her hands out to the shining tear in reality that was still showing the parlor of Cecil's New York residence. She seemed to grab the ragged, sparking edges of the opening and pulled them together like she was closing curtains. The tear became a lightning bolt, ten feet tall, waving from side to side as if it was trying to escape from her grip. Janya bowed her head and pushed her hands out again in a reversal of the curtain-closing movement.

The opening now showed the very familiar desk in Dorothy's study. They were facing the door so they saw when Trafalgar walked in and nearly tripped on her feet when she saw the portal.

"Crumbs," Dorothy growled. "Close it. Close it now!"

Cecil looked at her. "You said you wanted to go home..."

"Dorothy?" Trafalgar said, freed from her initial stupor and hurrying around the desk.

"Close it!" Dorothy snapped.

Janya pulled the edges together again just before Trafalgar reached it.

Dorothy breathed out a sigh of relief and shook her head. "Blast. I meant *London*, you dolt. Just in general. Not in my bloody office!"

"But you said *home*," Cecil said again. "London *is* your home, it's where your damn office is. It's not our fault you were unclear."

Dorothy shook her head. She was mostly irritated by the fact he wasn't entirely wrong. She should have realized Trafalgar and the Society would have taken over the townhouse as soon as she vacated the premises. Discovering they were lying in wait was actually a good thing, and could have saved her from walking into a trap. The only problem was that she didn't have an alternate location. The Inkwell always had at least a few apprentices hanging around researching something or another. It would be easier to slip out past them, however.

"The Inkwell," she said. "Upstairs, in the research section."

Janya nodded and focused, then opened the portal a third time. The only light in the library was coming from the portal itself, which was a good sign. Dorothy nodded her thanks and stepped forward. Cecil held up a hand to stop her.

"Whatever is going on with you and the rest of the Society, I want you to know you've got friends. A'right? No matter what."

Dorothy pursed her lips and looked at Janya, then down at her shoes.

"Mr. Dubourne, you've been a tremendous help to me, so I hesitate to say this. But I feel I must be blunt in order to get my message across. I loathe you. I believe you and these women are corrupting influences on each other, and it's only a matter of time before the rest of the Society is forced to band together to put an end to your back-alley shenanigans. I am only relying on you because I have literally no one else I can call and time is of the essence."

His smile remained in place, but she could see a tightening around his eyes that betrayed his true feelings. He cleared his throat and gestured grandly at the portal.

"Then for your sake, I hope you're never desperate and in need again."

"You and me both, Cecil."

She didn't even glance at Janya as she stepped through the portal and into the dark, stuffy upper room of the Mnemosyne Society's library. The portal immediately closed behind her and the room was cast into a deep, blinding darkness. Dorothy held her breath and listened for evidence she wasn't alone. A few seconds later, she heard it coming from the shelves to her right.

"Whatever it was, it's gone now." Whispered, only slightly terrified.

"You don't know that. Maybe it was something arriving."

Dorothy walked toward the hushed voices. As she got closer, she saw a coat which had been thrown over something very lantern-shaped, with dim light spilling out from the bottom.

"I think I hear footsteps."

She was close enough to whip the coat from the lantern, casting light down the aisle between two shelves. The girls huddled there screamed. One buried her face into the other's chest and, to her credit, the taller of the two leaned forward in a protective stance. Or as protective as she could muster with her blouse off and her skirts tucked up around her waist. The other girl was even more naked, and Dorothy regretted interrupting their tryst.

The fighter blinked and leaned closer. "Lady Boone...?"

She recognized them as well: Myra Halfpenny and Susan McAlister.

The three women stared at each other for a long moment. It was clear the girls knew Dorothy wasn't exactly a favored member of the Society at the moment, but finding them in this predicament - and their own reverence for everything she'd done for them in the past - made it awkward for them to speak up. Dorothy was also very reluctant to use the girls' relationship as blackmail material or leverage to gain their help. She didn't want to make something beautiful into a sordid situation.

"I am content with agreeing this never happened," Dorothy finally said.

Myra looked at Susan, who was still cowering against her. There was an almost imperceptible nod between the two before Myra looked at Dorothy again.

"All right."

"Is there anyone else downstairs?"

Myra said, "No," at the same time Susan shook her head and said, "Uh-uh."

"Okay, good." Dorothy draped the coat over the lantern again, backing away into the shadows. "Carry on, ladies. Enjoy your evening."

She fled before they could change their minds. They were both apprenticed with Cora, which meant they were likely infected with a strong moral compass and an urge to do the right thing. At the moment she knew they would decide the "right thing" was to take Dorothy into their custody and let the rest of the Society know she'd made an appearance.

Dorothy passed through the empty downstairs of the Inkwell and threw open the front door. It was chillier in London than it had been in Paris, giving her a moment of shock as she crossed to the front gate. She was already mentally planning her next move, was already inside the taxicab heading toward Threnody's place to beg for weapons she could use to retake her home, so it took her longer than she wanted to admit before she realized she wasn't alone.

She turned and looked back down the empty street. "Please tell me you haven't been following me long."

"Just since Paris." Ivy Sever's voice seemed to come from directly in front of Dorothy, but she knew the woman could be deceptive in that regard. "Cora asked me to keep an eye on Cecil and his girls. Not one person in that house is perceptive enough to realize they have an unwanted guest. Well... the maid is. But she don't mind a ghost so long as I don't hog the covers."

Dorothy couldn't help but smile. "I swear I heard you wink."

"When you're invisible, you work with what you have. Anyway, they've been as boring as chores, so when Cecil said you called for help... how could I resist? Lady Boone in need of assistance? That's always a quick road to an interesting couple of days. So I guess you're on the outs with the rest of the Society, hm?"

"So it would seem. I wish I could explain my position to you, but I'm in a bit of a hurry. So let's not beat around the bush. Are you going to let me go, or will we have to fight?"

"From what I overheard from Cecil and Janya, you haven't got a single friend left," Ivy said. "I've never really been a fan of people ganging up on one person. You've never steered me wrong before. And honestly, I owe you for what happened between us and Maud Keaton."

"You don't owe me~"

"Shush. I'm not going to turn you in or fight you."

"Really?"

"Everyone needs an ally," Ivy said.

Dorothy smiled. "Well, then. I believe I have just the task for you."

CHAPTER SIX

TRAFALGAR STARED at the empty space that had moments ago been some kind of tear in reality. She had seen Dorothy, Cecil Dubourne, and one of his apprentices standing on just the other side of a flickering golden archway in what seemed to be some kind of park. They appeared to be standing on grass, which didn't make sense since the office was above ground level. But if it had been a portal to somewhere else, most likely to France, then maybe things like that didn't matter.

Cora and Violet had rushed into the room when they heard her shout, but they hadn't been fast enough to see the portal before it closed. Mere moments ago, they had uncovered the artifact behind Dorothy's shed. It was covered by a tarp but otherwise unprotected and unremarkable. Ordinary stone at first glance, but shining their torch on it revealed seams of a reflective element threaded throughout. Trafalgar had headed upstairs to check Dorothy's books for any references that might explain what the object was or where it came from when she was distracted by the spectacle behind the desk.

"None of the apprentices have the ability to open a portal like that," Cora said once Trafalgar explained what had happened. "At least none who have revealed it."

Violet said, "I never saw anything like that when we were with Keaton, either. Anyone who could open a door from Paris to London would've been top tier for all kinds of jobs."

"For good reason," Trafalgar said. "There were always hints of secondary manifestations. We hadn't heard of anything like that from the rest of the apprentices."

"And we haven't seen much evidence of it," Cora said. "Most of the girls lost their powers completely. Those who retained them were at least a little diminished."

Trafalgar waved her hand in the air. "It's a debate for another time. For all we know, the woman with Cecil could have been using some kind of artifact. The only pertinent fact is that Dorothy was trying to use a portal to come back to London. We have to assume she may have chosen a secondary location and is already back."

Violet said, "She is. The Inkwell."

"Excellent. The bell is on the cat. At least she won't be able to sneak up on us. Is she coming this way, dear?"

"No," Violet said. "She's moving west. I can't imagine why. I'll keep tabs on her."

Trafalgar nodded and tried to think of any safe harbors Dorothy might have in that part of London. "The artifact we uncovered in the garden is the only thing that matters. She can't go back in time without it, which means whatever plan she's concocted is just pointlessly moving pieces on a chessboard. We can still stop her, get her help. We need to secure the artifact to ensure she can't get her hands on it."

Cora said, "That will be difficult since we just determined she can hop over to Paris and back in the blink of an eye."

"I don't think that matters much, as long as she doesn't know where it is. We need somewhere completely secure, a place she won't think to even check."

Violet said, "There's one option that's pretty foolproof. We could just destroy it."

Trafalgar said, "Bite your tongue. We can't destroy something so precious. It could be the last relic of a dead civilization. And if it actually does contain the secret to time travel, it might be the most important find of the past century."

"But time travel is dangerous, and can only lead to horrific abuses," Cora said. "It's impossible for it to stay out of the wrong hands because literally no one should be entrusted with such power. There are no right hands for this. I think Violet is right. The only way to ensure Dorothy can't go forward with her plan is to destroy the artifact now or we will, without question, regret it later."

Trafalgar pursed her lips. "I understand your point. But it's an action that cannot be undone. I don't want to take such a drastic step unless it's absolutely necessary. We will keep guards on it around the clock until Dorothy has been taken into custody, and then we will have a full debate about its eventual fate. Can everyone live with that?"

Cora and Violet looked at each other. Violet nodded first, and then Cora did as well.

"Excellent." She stretched her arms out to either side and considered their next move. "We'll take shifts. Love, I'm sorry, but we're going to need you to keep tabs on Dorothy as long as she's at large. You can rest if you confirm she's a safe distance away, and~"

"No," Violet said. "We can't let down our guard. We just confirmed she can get from Paris to this very room faster than Cora and I could get here from downstairs. It won't matter if she's right outside or somewhere in North America. I'll remain alert for as long as I can."

Trafalgar wanted to argue, but objectively knew she was right. Still, it was a lot to ask.

"It's my duty as a member of the Society," Violet said, sensing her wife's hesitation. "Besides, my discomfort will only spur you on to capture her as quickly as possible."

"You're correct about that. Very well. Cora, get word out. I want this house filled with as many Society members in good standing as you can round up on short notice. Where is the artifact now?"

Cora gestured toward the door. "Downstairs. We left it in the dining room."

Trafalgar nodded. "The best place for it will be the vault. Dorothy has that place so secured that even she will have a hard time breaking into it without causing a fuss. Sadie maintained her speed, didn't she?" Cora nodded. "Have her come and check it out for any other landmines that might have been placed in the past few years. I won't have anyone else caught off-guard like Alma and Florence were."

"I'll start calling immediately."

Cora stepped around the desk to use Dorothy's phone, and Trafalgar moved out of the way to give her room. She put a hand on Violet's elbow and guided her toward the door.

"Are you sure you're okay with this constant vigilance?"

"I'll tell you if I start flagging, but I'm fine for now. I can monitor her movements without too much exertion. Sort of like watching something from the corner of my eye. I'll notice if it changes in a direction that causes alarm, or drops off the map entirely."

"That's all we can ask of you." She kissed Violet's cheek and squeezed her arm. "In the meantime, we'll..." She turned her head toward the door, then stepped out into the hall. One of the planks that had once been the townhouse's front door had dropped onto the tile and was quickly silenced. There were no follow-up shouts of greeting.

"Trav?" Violet asked. "What's wrong?"

"Someone just came in through the front door."

Violet looked downstairs. "I don't see~ Ivy Sever...? Do you really think she's back?"

"She has a habit of popping up, so to speak, at the most inopportune times. I can't remember the last time we encountered her."

"Twenty-seven," Cora said from behind the desk. "She helped out the Keepings with that tomb-robber in Cairo."

"That's right." Trafalgar started downstairs. "Ivy? Are you there? If you're concerned for Dorothy's well-being, I want to assure you that we're not hostiles. We're her friends. We're trying to help her, but it's... it's a complicated time right now."

"You have a funny way of helping your friends."

Judging by where her voice came from, Ivy was farther into the house than Trafalgar had expected. Violet had followed Trafalgar downstairs and was pressed against her from behind. She slipped her hand between Trafalgar's arm and torso, then extended her arm straight forward and pointed to an empty spot near the parlor door. As soon as her finger settled, she moved it to the left. Stopped. Went back to the right.

"Damn," Ivy chuckled. "I forgot about your little bloodhound. How are things, Mrs. Rhys?"

"Everything is fantastical, Miss Sever." Violet's voice was right next to Trafalgar's ear, and she repressed a shudder at the feel of breath on her cheek. She was far more accustomed to this position having a far more intimate context, so she struggled to keep her focus. Her finger wavered, then snapped back. "You can save your energy with the theatrics. I'll always know where you are."

"Your wife is treating me like a threat, Trafalgar. I'm still part of the gang, right? Mnemosyne Society pals, all the way."

"You've always been a wild variable, Ivy. You once used Dorothy's trust against her. I'd like to be absolutely certain of your motives before I let my guard down."

"I guess I can't hold that against you." Violet's finger followed Ivy as she moved toward the base of the stairs. "I haven't exactly proven myself as trustworthy, hm? You're right to be wary. But I think you have bigger things to worry about. Like if your wife is so focused on keeping track of me while I'm faffing around, what might have slipped her mind?"

Trafalgar tensed. Violet slapped her free hand down on Trafalgar's shoulder.

"Oh, blast it! She's here!"

Before Trafalgar could move, the invisible thief and assassin slammed into her and knocked her down. It was the second time that evening she'd been knocked off her feet, and it was humiliating both times. She put her hands up in front of her and felt the unseen curve of a shoulder, then the thin column of Ivy's neck. She squeezed both and tried to shove her up and off, but Ivy sent a hard, sharp jab into Trafalgar's gut and knocked the wind out of her.

"Cora!" Violet called, squirming to get out from underneath Trafalgar. "Dorothy is here! She's downstairs! You must stop her!"

Cora came out of the office at a dead run. She flew down the stairs, realizing the danger as Violet cried out, "Careful!" but it was too late. Ivy only had to shoot out her arm to trip Cora, who plunged forward and landed face down on the bottom steps before sliding the rest of the way to the floor of the entry hall.

Trafalgar planted her feet and shoved forward. Ivy was in a terrible, awkward position and even breathless it wasn't difficult to gain the upper hand on her. Keeping it, however...

Once they were back in a standing position, Ivy spun Trafalgar and slammed her hard against the wall. Violet jumped onto Ivy's back and put her in a choke hold.

"Dorothy," Trafalgar wheezed. "I have her. Violet, go. Stop Dorothy. She mustn't get the artifact."

She saw the indecision in Violet's eyes, but still she released Ivy and ran. Trafalgar focused on grappling with an enemy she couldn't see. She closed her eyes and let her other senses tell her where Ivy was. She grabbed Ivy's throat again and, when she brought her hand up to block a punch, managed to get a solid grip on one wrist. She spun them both like they were dancing, swept her leg in front of her, and felt Ivy go heavy in her arms, threatening to pull her down. She let go just before she was tipped over, and she heard Ivy hit the stairs below as hard as Cora had moments earlier.

"Gossamer bitch," Trafalgar rasped.

She moved down, intending to check Cora for injuries, but she froze when she heard a gunshot from the dining room.

Dorothy ran. It didn't matter where she ran, only that she aimed herself in a direction that led away from the Threadneedle Street townhouse. Trafalgar's wife would most likely be checking in. As long as they thought she was far away, their guard would be down. The people she passed looked at her in shock and curiosity, but she wouldn't let herself be distracted by their gawping. Already her lungs were burning and cold sweat had beaded on her hot forehead. Too much time spent hunkered over books and nowhere near enough time exercising, preparing, readying herself for a confrontation. If she was thrown up against a true enemy, someone unlike Trafalgar who wouldn't have any qualms about hurting her, she would have been in quite dire straits indeed.

She hated how much of her plan hinged on Ivy Sever. Each year that the woman spent in her invisible state seemed to change her in subtle ways. Their brief conversation was enough for Dorothy to be certain the woman she'd once known was gone forever. Ivy was a ghost, a specter, a remnant of who she'd once been when she walked the world as a visible person. Dorothy supposed if a person got used to no one seeing them, to being ignored in a crowd, it would do all sorts of horrible things to their mind, to their personality.

She couldn't think about that now. Perhaps there would be something they could do later, once the world was set right. If Dorothy could travel in time to save Beatrice, certainly she could do the same to find a cure for Ivy's condition. Or, hell, she could ensure that it never happened at all. Why not spare her the hell of invisibility if it was within her power?

So much was within her power. Lost lives restored. Battles waged again with foreknowledge of the enemy's tactics and movements. There was no limit to what she could do with the artifact and Beatrice Sek at her side.

First, however, this plan had to go absolutely perfectly. The timing was ridiculously complex, but Janya had been willing to try it. Dorothy couldn't risk slowing down to check her watch. She had to trust she was running at the right speed, going the right way, and that Janya and Ivy were reliable. She kept a count in her head to distract her from the pain in her body. It felt like her heart was going to explode out of her chest. Her lungs burned. The sweat on her forehead had now dripped down into her eyes and she blinked it away, refusing to be blinded.

Ten seconds. Now seven. Now three.

A portal opened in front of her. Too far away. Crumbs, she was going too slow! She growled, shouted, and found the reserves to put on an extra burst of speed. Through the portal she could see a second one was already standing open and waiting for her. Janya peeked around the edge, standing between the two openings, and ducked out of the way so Dorothy wouldn't collide with her.

Dorothy entered the first portal. Her boots pounded two heavy steps on the floorboards of a hardwood floor in a New York library. She passed through the second portal and slammed into one of the chairs in her own dining room. She stumbled, fell against the wall, and exhaled sharply as she grabbed the edge of the table to catch her breath. Her pulse pounded in her temples. Her face, as well as her lungs, felt like she'd set a match to them.

But there! Right there on the dining room table, by sheer luck, she saw the artifact. She slipped her arm into the center of the ring and lifted it. Now all she had to do was carry it into the portal and let Janya close it behind her. Unfortunately the artifact was just a bit too heavy and her arms refused to cooperate. She lifted, cried out, and collapsed down onto the table again.

"Damn and blast it," she exhaled, panting with her cheek against the stone. "Just two more blasted steps. Come on!"

She heard shouting elsewhere in the house. Ivy and her distraction. It wouldn't last forever. Dorothy bared her teeth and straightened her back, her muscles crying out in protest as she tried to lift the stone and turn at the same time.

"Stop!" Violet Rhys slammed into her and Dorothy fell again, this time almost crushing her arm under the artifact.

"Let me go, you foolish woman!"

"We're doing this for your own good, Boone."

Dorothy dug her elbow into Violet's stomach but still the blasted woman wouldn't let her go. Dorothy had to release her grip on the artifact to brace both hands on the table and push off to propel herself backward. She pushed Violet into the wall, which stunned her enough that Dorothy was able to get free and turned to face her.

Violet's shoulder exploded in a flash of red. They both cried out, both shocked by the delayed sound of a gunshot, and then Violet collapsed back against the wall as she clapped a hand over the wound. Blood poured through her fingers and stained her blouse as her legs gave out and gravity slowly pulled her down the wall into a sitting position.

Dorothy spun around and saw Janya aiming a gun through the portal. "Are you coming or not?" Janya asked.

"You idiot!" Dorothy said. "What have you~"

Her question was cut off by a devastating blow across her jaw. It knocked her completely sideways, feet off the floor and sprawled on the table. She saw a flash of Trafalgar's face, the whites of her wide eyes and teeth bared in rage, one arm raised above her head in the first swing of what was sure to be a bone-shattering blow.

The blow never came. Instead, a very weak voice said, "Trav..." and all the fury faded from Trafalgar's face. She turned and looked over her shoulder, let out a weak cry, and abandoned Dorothy to drop to her knees next to her bleeding wife. Dorothy pushed herself up and dropped onto the floor. She saw Janya taking aim again and held up her hand to stop her. Janya raised an eyebrow but lowered the weapon. Dorothy stared, instinctively knowing she shouldn't say the words that had formed in her mind but knowing she couldn't stop them from coming out.

"If she doesn't make it," she said, "consider what you would do to have her back."

Trafalgar didn't look at her. "If you speak to me again, I swear I will end your life."

Dorothy reached for the artifact but stopped when she heard the click of a shotgun from the hall.

"I will try to shoot to maim," Cora said, her voice slurring just a bit, "but I'm not that good of a shot. At this point I don't care. Leave it."

"Cora," Dorothy whispered. "Please. It's Beatrice."

Through the portal, Dorothy saw Cecil arrive. He looked stunned, his face pale as he assessed the situation. He saw the blood on the wall, Trafalgar, Cora Hyde with a gun. He looked at Dorothy and pressed his lips together. Dorothy understood what was about to happen and held his gaze, forcing him to look at her as he gestured for Janya to close the portal. Janya shrugged, put down her gun, and swept her hand across the opening.

The portal closed. Dorothy, exhausted and defeated, held at gunpoint in her own dining room, closed her eyes and raised her hands, surrendering to the inevitable.

Trafalgar lost minutes. Perhaps as much as an hour. She could only see her hand on top of Violet's, their fingers smeared with blood. She watched Violet's face and felt her heart seize whenever her eyes drifted shut for too long or her breathing seemed a bit too labored. She heard movement behind her. Cora speaking, Dorothy saying something only to be quickly silenced and led from the room. She heard herself say, "Help... get her help..." but didn't know if she'd said it before or after Cora left.

"Stopped her, Trav," Violet murmured, her lips barely moving.

"Sh, don't talk." Trafalgar cupped Violet's cheek with her free, unbloodied hand. "Don't waste your energy. I'm here. I'm right here."

Violet grunted and rolled her head to the side. She was deathly pale, and her whole face shined with sweat. She forced her eyes open and looked at Trafalgar without seeming to see her.

"Thank you for giving me... everything."

"Please don't talk like that. Please." Trafalgar's eyes burned. She thought of Desmond, of Abraham Strode, and Beatrice. Beautiful souls taken before their time. She couldn't bear for that to happen the woman she loved. She thought of Dorothy's hateful words and knew she was right. She would do anything to prevent this moment, to undo this pain.

"I can help."

Trafalgar turned toward the new voice. She hadn't heard anyone enter and quickly understood why; Edith Bowles was standing in front of a portal. She was one of Cecil's apprentices and had the ability to create golems. She could also heal minor ailments. She was rubbing her hands together, her brow knit with worry, trembling with the desire to dash forward but stopping herself until she was asked.

"This was your doing," Trafalgar snapped. "If you bastards hadn't helped her~"

"Cees understands that," Edith interrupted. "That's why I'm here. He thinks things have gotten out of control. I can help her, but I have to... it has to be soon. She's going quick. Please, Trafalgar, we just want to try to help make this right."

Trafalgar swallowed a lump in her throat the size of an egg. She looked at Violet, whose eyes had closed again. Her lips were slack, and her skin looked gray.

"Do it," Trafalgar said as she rose from the floor.

Edith practically pounced into the space where Trafalgar had just been sitting. She placed her right hand over the wound and then covered it with her left. Blood immediately seeped around her fingers but she ignored it and bowed her head. Trafalgar watched and physically felt walls inside of her beginning to crumble. If Violet died, if she had to look at her wife's dead body, she knew they would shatter and she would instantly become a different person. She wrapped her arms around her body, hugging herself without regard for the blood she was smearing on her clothes, and waited.

Violet's slack lips trembled and then pressed together. She frowned without opening her eyes like she was caught in a bad dream, then gasped and twitched violently.

"Trav?" she groaned.

"It's all right, Violet. She's helping you."

"Hurts. S'like fire."

Trafalgar's eyes filled with tears. "I know, my love."

Someone stepped out of the portal next to Trafalgar. She knew it was Cecil without looking; she still recognized his aftershave and *eau de toilette* after all these years.

"I know this don't make us square," he said under his breath. "I'll never be your friend, you probably never would've trusted me to have your back on a mission. But if... I let this happen... without at least trying to fix it, that would have made me your sworn enemy. And that would pretty much be the end of me. Couldn't have that."

Trafalgar didn't respond. She knew that Edith wasn't a miracle worker. The girl typically only healed headaches, cramps, other minor wounds. Even those took a lot out of her, left her weak and sickly. Trafalgar couldn't let her hopes get too high for something of this magnitude. She watched as the color returned to Violet's face, even as Edith swayed and her arms started to tremble. The blood didn't seem to be flowing anymore, but the stain already covered one entire half of Violet's blouse.

Cora came running into the house with a man in tow. The man was short and bald and had a medical bag swinging from one arm. He and Cora both stopped at the doorway to the dining room as she took in the tableau before them, then found Trafalgar and seemed to blink out of her stupor.

"I brought a doctor."

"Thank God," Edith moaned. "I th-think I've done everything I can for her, but there's still... she's not entirely... um..." She coughed and fell to the side as if she lacked the ability to remain upright. She coughed again, and this time blood spotted her bottom lip. Cecil went to her, helped her up and let her lean against his side as the doctor moved to examine his patient. Edith looked like death warmed over, but now so did Violet, and that was a marked improvement on her condition just moments ago.

Trafalgar stared at Edith until the girl felt her gaze and looked up. "Thank you."

"She's not out of the woods yet," Edith said. "I did everything I felt comfortable doing, but with muscles and tendons, you want it to heal as naturally as possible. Otherwise things go wrong."

"You tried, at great cost to yourself. That is worth everything to me."

Edith nodded and slumped heavier against Cecil's side.

After quick, frantic work, the doctor turned to look at the small crowd gathered behind him in the kitchen. He sighed and took off his glasses.

"I'll be able to help her. I can stabilize her condition. But I need the room. Please, if you would be so kind..."

Cecil gestured at the portal and Trafalgar nodded. He stepped through and it closed behind him. Trafalgar idly wondered where Janya had been hiding while the portal was open, but decided not to waste too much mental energy on the question. The artifact was still on the dinner table, so she honestly couldn't care less about the blasted woman's location.

Cora put an arm around Trafalgar's shoulders and guided her out of the room. "Come on. Let's allow the doctor to do his job. I can have one of my girls take care of the artifact."

Trafalgar forced herself to look away from Violet and focused on the hallway in front of her. The further she got from the dining room, the clearer her thoughts became. Fear and panic gave way to anger, a pure rage she wasn't sure she'd ever felt before. Her body tensed and she stood up taller. Cora leaned away from her, feeling the shift in Trafalgar's posture. Trafalgar looked at her.

"Where is Dorothy Boone?"

CHAPTER SEVEN

DOROTHY WAS in the parlor on the ground floor. She was sat in a chair which had been taken from the study, with a sturdy wooden frame, and her wrists bound to the ornate arms. Her ankles were similarly bound to the legs of the chair, and another rope had been crossed over her chest in the form of an X to lash her to the back of the chair as well. No one in the room was willing to take any chances when it came to restraining a woman as sly and wily as Dorothy Boone.

And the room was quite full. Cora had sent up the alarm before she fled to get the doctor, and the other Society members in the house leapt into action. Susannah, Sadie, Helena, Emily, Mabel, Myra, Susan, Alice, Mary, Angel, Honour, the Read twins, and Albina were all crowded in the parlor. Some surrounded Dorothy in a ring, a dozen eyes fixed on her for any signs of escape. The rest were watching every potential point of entrance: the window, the doors, Alice was even monitoring the fireplace on the off-chance someone slipped in that way. A few of them had taken the time to cover the destroyed door with a plank of wood, doing their best to secure the house until it could be properly fixed.

The congregation parted when Cora and Trafalgar entered the room. Cora remained at the door, but Trafalgar marched forward. Dorothy could feel the pain, anger, and hatred emanating off her former friend like a physical wave, and braced herself to be punched the second she was within arm's reach. Trafalgar's clothes were smeared with blood.

Trafalgar stopped in front of Dorothy and stared down at her. For a moment it seemed like the entire crowded room was frozen in time. No one moved, not one foot shifted or breath was taken.

After an excruciating silence, Dorothy wet her lips. "I'm sorr~"

Trafalgar slapped her hard enough that Dorothy's head rocked sideways, hurting her neck. The ropes across her chest pulled tight and made it difficult for her to inhale. She settled back in the seat and worked her jaw back and forth since she couldn't rub the injured spot.

"Well. It seems to have cleared up that clicking sound that started after you punched me."

"Say it again."

Dorothy looked up at her. She tasted blood in her mouth. "What?"

Trafalgar's expression was flat, unreadable. "Say it again."

Dorothy swallowed. "I'm s~"

This time the slap was expected, but Trafalgar used her other hand. Dorothy's whole face stung, and her jaw really was still throbbing from the punch earlier.

"What are you apologizing for? Hm? For trying to trade Violet's life for Beatrice? For putting the woman I love in danger for your ridiculous fantasy?"

Dorothy looked away. "It was never my intention for anyone to be hurt. Is Violet all right?"

"That is the last time you're allowed to say her name," Trafalgar said. "That is the last time you can pretend you care about her well-being without being answered with some form of violence. Am I understood?"

"Mm," Dorothy said. "So she's alive. I truly am glad."

Trafalgar took a step back. She inhaled, let out her breath, and then looked up again once she had centered herself.

"Cecil Dubourne and his apprentices are no longer on your side. The artifact will be secured and you will never, ever see it again. Your allies are gone. In the morning, Cora and I will begin looking for an appropriate place for you to go in order to finally process your grief."

Dorothy closed her eyes and bowed her head, struggling to find a way to make them understand. Finally she looked up again.

"You know me, Trafalgar. Cora. You both know me well, trust me, believed in me when no one else did. Do you honestly think I would have dedicated most of the past decade to this mission if there was a chance it was impossible?"

"I think you would move heaven and earth to save someone you love," Cora said. "And I think sometimes you let your emotion get in the way of your better sense."

"We can change so much. Bring so much good."

Trafalgar leaned down so Dorothy was forced to look into her eyes. "Who are we to decide? What right do we have to make that choice for the entire world? All we can do is fight now, today, and hope we're making the right decisions for the future. Just like everyone else."

Dorothy shouted, "But we can do so much more!"

"And where would we stop? Hm? You seem to think stopping magic from being used in the War is enough. Save Beatrice, wipe your hands, job done. But we've got this amazing artifact, so why not just hop back and save Desmond, too? You can go back even further and prevent the Russian flu, or save the *Titanic*. What's to stop you from changing every single past event you disagree with? The entire world rewritten to Dorothy Boone's standards."

"Would it be so awful?" Dorothy said softly. "Isn't that all any of us are doing anyway? Trying to build a world we can bear to live in?"

"And the moment someone figures out what you're doing, or gains access to the artifact? What then? What atrocities could we be responsible for? Your entire plan hinges around preventing this very thing from happening! You want to prevent foolish people from using power they have no right toying with. The artifact is far too powerful to be used by anyone, for any purpose, no matter how altruistic it may seem at the time."

"I have to do this, Trafalgar. You won't talk me out of it, not when I'm so close."

Trafalgar straightened and shook her head. "You will be monitored all night. There will be at least five women with you at all times. If you decide to sleep, you will do so seated in the chair. If you require the facilities, I suggest you overcome any embarrassment you might have of doing it with an audience."

"I understand," Dorothy said. "I'm your prisoner."

"It's my sincere hope that one day you'll thank us for this."

Dorothy narrowed her eyes. "That would require speaking to any of you again. Especially after the hypocrisy you've just shown. You're suddenly against the use of supernatural measures when magic just saved the woman you love."

Trafalgar's jaw tightened. When she spoke again, Dorothy could hear the barely contained rage in her voice. "My wife was nearly killed by a bullet fired in New York. She would never have been in danger were it not for you or your blasted magic."

"Let me end it. Let me go back and prevent magic from ever being unleashed on this world."

"Pandora's box is open," Trafalgar said. "We've cleaned up as much of the mess as we can. Tragically, it cost us the life of someone very dear to us. We can only do our best to carry on and make her sacrifice mean something."

Dorothy lowered her head, finally convinced Trafalgar was never going to see her perspective.

"Will you do one thing before you leave?" Dorothy asked. "Reach into one of the pockets of my coat. Any pocket, it doesn't matter. There's no trick, no trap, no weapon waiting to snare you. There's just something I want you to see."

Trafalgar looked at Cora. They both stepped forward and Cora took a defensive position in the event Dorothy did have something up her sleeve. Trafalgar chose the most accessible pocket and reached in. Her expression gave away the fact she was clearly expecting some kind of weapon, but the wariness was quickly replaced by confusion as she pulled her hand out and opened it to reveal she was holding a small pile of dirt.

"What is this?"

"Dirt. Soil. Earth." Dorothy shrugged. "It's been appearing in my pockets since the Void event. Since Beatrice was... lost to us. This is proof she is still here, somewhere. She's urging me on."

"It's dirt, Dorothy." Trafalgar turned her hand over and let it fall to the floor. She brushed it from her palm with angry swipes. "Honestly, given the state of this place, I'm hardly surprised it's gotten into your clothing. The fact you believe it's a sign from Beatrice is just one more sign that we should have done this years ago."

Dorothy sighed and sagged against the seat. "She would have gone to the ends of the Earth for you, Trafalgar."

"I would never have asked her to. And if something happened to me, and I somehow saw that you'd thrown away so much of your life to the foolish pursuit of something that cannot happen... it would break my heart. If this is truly the last time we speak, I want to thank you for everything I've gained from knowing you. My life is infinitely better for having you in it. I'm sorry our time together has to end. But the events of this day have proven that we can never be partners again. I hope one day you will consider me a friend again."

Dorothy remained silent and kept her head turned away. Eventually she looked back and saw that Trafalgar and Cora had left the room and the Society women had once again closed ranks around her. She squirmed to sit up straighter and squared her shoulders.

"Who is up for a game of musical chairs, hm...?"

Florence was still recuperating in the master bedroom, so once the doctor was finished, Trafalgar had Violet transferred to the room which had once been hers. She had no idea of the time; it was dark outside, but she didn't know if they had minutes or hours until sunrise. She asked Angel Tuffin to carry Violet upstairs and gently place her in the bed. Angel was a giant, strong enough to punch someone through a wall if she got the urge, but her hands were tender as they tucked the blankets around Violet's shoulders and moved a pillow under her head. Violet didn't resist being moved around, but her face had the slackness of a deep sleep rather than anything more alarming.

Trafalgar thanked Angel for her help and then stretched out on the mattress to lay next to her wife. She held her breath so she could hear Violet's slow but steady inhale, the strong exhale, the proof she really was going to be okay despite the bruises on her shoulder and the darkened stains on her blouse. The wound was mercifully out of sight under gauze, but Trafalgar still felt she could see it burned on the back of her eyelids. The way the blood had gushed between her fingers...

She had tried to wash her hands after she talked to Dorothy, but she still felt she could see it caked into the nails. So very Shakespearian, the indelible stain, and she squeezed her hands into fists in an attempt to stop thinking about what might or might not be lingering in the lines of her palm.

Even now, she didn't quite understand how Violet Rhys had come into her life. There had been no pursuit, no courtship. Trafalgar wasn't looking for a relationship, even though her arrangement with Dorothy and Beatrice had of course been put on pause. But one day this gorgeous Welsh woman with the curls and the Cheshire smile appeared in her path, and suddenly being without her was not an option. They first slept together in this bed. When she and Dorothy's paths diverged, Trafalgar moved out and set up a flat with Violet.

Their arrangement hadn't been smooth - there had been arguments and heated discussions, the usual tremors of two bodies learning to share a small space and bumping into each other - but Trafalgar could barely remember them now. She only remembered waking up with a blanket drawn across her lap and her book set aside. She remembered decorating the dining room and learning to bake a cake for Violet's first birthday they were together.

She remembered the discussion of starting their own business, trying to decide on a name.

"Rhys Tracking & Investigation has a much better ring than Trafalgar & Violet. Or Violet & Trafalgar, if you prefer. Surnames are key."

Violet shrugged. "I can't argue with that. But that would make it mine. I want it to be ours, in no uncertain terms. Equal partners."

"But I don't have a surname. I never have."

"Well..." Violet sat up straighter. "What if you did?"

Trafalgar looked at her. They had been together for over a year, but neither had broached this subject even in passing, or in jest.

"You can't mean marriage."

"Why can't I?"

Trafalgar laughed. "There are quite a few disqualifications I can think of."

"Then we'll make it unofficial. But a name? A person can call themselves anything. Hell, Dorothy Boone gave herself a damn title! Why can't you decide your name is Trafalgar Rhys?" Trafalgar noticed then that Violet's hands were shaking. She put hers on top of them. "I'm sorry," Violet said, shaking her head. "I've never asked anything like this before. I've never thought about it, either. I've never cared for anyone enough for it to be a possibility. But I think I'd like it if you had my name."

Trafalgar leaned in and kissed Violet's lips. "And I believe it is a name I would be honored to take as my own."

She closed her eyes to blink away a tear and kept them closed. She felt herself slipping, though she wouldn't call what happened next sleep. She was aware of movement on the staircase, people pausing on the landing to speak softly before continuing on their way.

When she opened her eyes, light was coming in through the window. The house was still and quiet. And Violet was watching her. They smiled at each other.

Violet touched Trafalgar's lips with her hand. "I remember this bed." Her voice was soft but there was a strength in it that hadn't been there the last time she'd spoken.

"It's quite an important landmark. Much history was made here."

"Mm." Violet's eyes drifted shut. "It hurts, Trav. But nowhere near as much as it should. You saved me. Thank you."

Trafalgar shook her head. "I didn't do anything. You owe a great thanks to Edith Bowles and... crumbs. I never got the doctor's name. Or if I did, I forgot it."

"Someone will know it," Violet assured her. "We can thank him properly. What did I miss?"

Trafalgar briefly recapped Dorothy's capture. "Before I came up here, Cora told me that Sadie took the artifact somewhere secure. She can't get to it."

"And what happened to.. to Ivy...? The invisible woman."

"Gone again." Trafalgar tried to keep the irritation out of her voice. "By the time anyone thought to secure her, she had already regained consciousness and fled."

Violet closed her eyes. "I'm not sure~"

"Stop, stop," Trafalgar said. "I know most of the time it's second nature, but it takes something from you. Right now you need to use all your energy to heal."

Violet scooted closer, hissing as the move tugged at her bandages. Trafalgar met her in the middle and guided Violet's head to her shoulder.

"I found you because of magic," Violet said. "I would have been a different person. You would have remained in Africa."

"We found each other because we were meant to know one another. No matter what happened in the world, we were bound to be together."

Violet murmured softly. "Tell me a different story about how we met."

Trafalgar thought. She decided to ignore the part of her story that involved being taken from Ethiopia and brought to England without consent. It was less messy to just assume she was destined to one day make her way to this city.

"Without magic, I wouldn't have had a purpose in London. No serviceable skills, barely speaking the language. I would have been forced to steal in order to survive. Eventually I would meet a young woman with a name like a flower and a smile twice as beautiful. I would steal twice as much food so I could share it with her. So we would meet even sooner."

"But we would be living on the street."

Trafalgar said, "Ah, there are worse fates when you're with the person you love."

"Mm." Her voice was fading. "I love you, Trav."

"I love you, Violet." She kissed the blonde curls. "Rest. I'll be here when you wake."

Violet murmured something that Trafalgar didn't hear and drifted back to sleep.

Dorothy didn't try to sleep. It seemed like a lost cause, and she dreaded any dreams her subconscious might produce in her current state. She was surrounded by women from the Society. Some of whom she'd been close to considering friends, if not protégés, when they were first liberated from Maud Keaton's grasp. Now she didn't doubt they would cause her grievous bodily harm if she tried to escape.

She'd been so close. If she'd just secured the artifact better. If she'd been quicker, better at deception. If Trafalgar hadn't known her well enough to anticipate her moves. She should have just remained in 1910 and done the proper investigative work to find Durocher and the other practitioners. But she'd been so concerned it would take her too long, that she would end up running out of time... coming back had been the smarter idea. She thought she could take as much time as she needed here before she went back with everything she needed in her mind.

She should have known the plan was doomed as soon as she discovered she'd overshot her return by a year. A *year*. What if her return to the past was equally skewed? What if she went through all of this madness only to go back and arrive too late?

I'm so sorry, Beatrice. You deserved better than me.

She was certain that sleep would never come, so she studied the women assigned to watch her. She knew them all to some degree or another. She'd fought a couple of them, back when they were known by the moniker 'the Forty Elephants.' But now they were all fine upstanding gentlewomen, thanks in part to her. Didn't they owe her some kind of loyalty? Or at least a single favor. Even if she could isolate one of them, she had no idea which would be the most receptive to her pleas of compassion.

They were very good guards, she noted. They changed shifts one at a time, at the quarter-hour mark. When they weren't on-duty, they curled up in comfortable spots around the room so they could be summoned with the slightest shout or raised voice. There were fourteen women crammed into the room with her, and she had to assume that at least a half dozen of them considered her an enemy. She couldn't turn enough to make a difference.

The twins, Phoebe and Pamela Read, were on a shift together sometime after two in the morning. Instead of taking up a position between Dorothy and the door, they knelt on the floor in front of her and reached out to take her hands. Dorothy tensed.

"What are you doing?"

Pamela smiled and brushed her thumb over the back of Dorothy's fingers. "Our power is to sing harmonies that cause reactions in others."

"We thought rather than threatening you, we could calm you down."

"Relax you."

"Soothe you."

Dorothy tried to pull her hands away but the ropes prevented her. She still tried to angle her body away from them. "Thank you, but I think I'll pass."

"Just relax," Phoebe said.

"It will make tonight and whatever tomorrow brings easier for everyone involved."

Dorothy looked past them at her other jailers, Susan and Myra were the closest. "You're just going to let them do this?"

Susan shrugged. "They do it for us all the time. Helps a lot."

Angel, leaning against the doorframe, said, "Got me through a bout of insomnia a few years back. I still wouldn't've been able to sleep if it weren't for these two."

One of the twins said, "Just relax."

Her sister said, "It will all be fine."

"I don't need~"

Dorothy wasn't even aware when one of the girls started to sing. She just heard the song and the words of argument died in her throat. She tensed, fighting against... she wasn't entirely sure what... as the other Read girl joined in. The room seemed to grow darker, but there was a light within the haze. Like seeing through smoke or a thick fog. Her lips parted but words were beyond her, and she felt the tension fade out of her arms as she slumped back against the cushion of the seat. The Read girls brushed their fingers over Dorothy's hand, writing patterns that made sense to some silent part of Dorothy's brain that responded to what their voices were doing.

"Hello, Dorothy."

She tensed. She wanted to open her eyes, but she was fairly sure her eyes were already open. The voice had come from behind her, but she didn't move to turn around.

"I won't look at you if you aren't really here. I refuse to see you only to have you leave again."

"Oh come on," Beatrice said, placing her hands on Dorothy's shoulders. "After everything you've done... all these years. You don't even want to say hello?"

Dorothy gave up and turned, tears burning her eyes. Beatrice smiled victoriously, and Dorothy couldn't help but return the smile. Beatrice wore her uniform, the white dress shirt open at the collar and the sleeves rolled up and pinned past her elbows. She cupped the gorgeous face and laughed when she actually felt warm, firm skin under her fingertips.

"Are you real?"

"No," Beatrice said. "I'm sorry. This is just, ah, something the Read twins can do. You're in an extremely deep hypnotic state. I'm your memories of Beatrice. I'm everything that you know deep down that she would want to say to you if she could."

Dorothy's smile wavered. "You're going to tell me to give up. After all this time, after all the signals you're still out there waiting for me to save you."

"I'm not telling you anything, Dorothy. I'm you, using Beatrice to tell you things you already know. And you know Trafalgar is right."

Dorothy closed her eyes. "I refuse to believe~"

"Darling." Beatrice stepped closer. "Think about what you're doing. Think about the consequences of success. You want to change the world so magic never wakes up. What if it means I never come to London? Or perhaps I never break into your home and wind up encased in stone. You want to create a version of the world where we never meet."

"I don't care. That's a sacrifice I'm willing to make." Her eyes flooded. "If having you alive somewhere in the world means being without you, then it's worth the pain."

Beatrice sighed and kissed Dorothy's lips. "You foolish woman... You can't change the past to fix the present. No one can, and anyone with the ability should be wise enough to stop themselves. I know you have the wisdom to stop yourself before you cause irreparable damage." She kissed Dorothy's cheek, embraced her, then whispered in her ear. "Do not become the villain of your own story, Dorothy Boone."

Dorothy embraced Beatrice. This had to be real. She could feel Beatrice in her arms, the muscles of her back, the smooth silk of her vest. She put her head down on Beatrice's shoulder and breathed deeply. She smelled the same, felt the same. For seven years she had dreamt of only this moment. Holding Beatrice, being held by her. Even if it was just a phantom conjured by her memories, wasn't that a relief as well? To know she hadn't forgotten such vital things?

"If I surrender, can I just stay here? I could be happy here."

"You would be comatose."

"Who needs the rest of the world?" Dorothy whispered.

Beatrice stroked Dorothy's hair. "The world needs *you*, Dorothy Boone." She stepped back and kissed Dorothy's forehead, soothing the furrows there. "There are threats and dangers still unknown that will need to be faced by you."

"Trafalgar and the Society~"

"Are incomplete without you."

"And I'm incomplete without you, Trix."

Beatrice sighed and ran her fingers through Dorothy's hair. "You don't have to give me up. You just can't go back in time and change the entire course of history to try and make a world where I'm still alive."

"It's the only way." Now the tears were rolling down Dorothy's face. "You don't think I exhausted my options? I chased down every myth, every rumor, every potential avenue."

"Where?"

"In my books, my records. The Mnemosyne library. The combined knowledge of every council member was gathered in those volumes. I found *nothing* but the account which led me to the ring artifact."

Beatrice nodded knowingly. "And when you found that lead, you chased it down immediately."

"Time was of the essence. I had to know if it was... if it was possible." The crease in her brow had returned. "And I found it. I-it worked. I went back to 1910 and I can do it again. I can change things."

"You found the artifact," Beatrice said softly. "And then you stopped looking."

"Of course I did. Why would I keep looking for something I'd already found?"

"You weren't thorough, love. You assumed you had your answer. The key to getting me back. You should have kept looking."

Dorothy shook her head. "No. You can't know that. Maybe I neglected a few shelves, but if you're telling the truth, you only know what I know. So you can't possibly know that I missed something." Realization hit her as soon as she saw Beatrice's knowing smile. "Unless I already know what I'm looking for. I know what can bring you back...?"

Beatrice only smiled at her.

"God, that's infuriating."

"I know." She rested her fingertips on Dorothy's temple. "The information is here, Dorothy. Along with the memory of how I look, sound, smell. The same wonderful mind that conjured me up holds the key. You just have to access it."

"Can you at least give me a hint?"

"You heard of a great many treasures during the War. But it was a time when travel was dangerous, expensive, and a luxury even you couldn't afford. You had to be very selective about which stories you pursued. Perhaps there was something you heard about during that period. Something you dismissed."

Dorothy shook her head. "There were so many stories coming in during that time. I can't... I-I don't remember."

The fog around them shifted into a hazy approximation of her office. Sunlight was passing through the window, and she saw a ghostly version of herself moving along the bookshelves.

"Not even a hint?"

"Maybe it was something you ignored because you heard one of your chief rivals was already interested in it. So you thought about it for a long time because even if it was fruitless in the end, you could beat her to the prize, and that would be worth the expense."

"Trafalgar?"

Beatrice narrowed her eyes. "Perhaps."

Dorothy growled through clenched teeth. "God, you are a pain."

"This is what talking to you is like for other people."

"Then I owe the world an apology!" Dorothy snapped. She rested her forehead against Beatrice's. "Please. I will burn down this world if that's what it takes to bring you back to me."

"I know, Dorothy."

Dorothy angled her face until she could press her lips to Beatrice's. They kissed tenderly, then with growing passion. Beatrice's arms relaxed and she ran her hands down Dorothy's back to her hips. Dorothy realized she was dressed as she had been in the real world: trousers and a button-down shirt with suspenders. As she kissed Beatrice, teaching parted lips with her tongue, she stepped back just far enough to shrug out of the suspenders and let the loops fall.

"If you were truly created my mind," Dorothy said, pressing a kiss to the corner of Beatrice's mouth, "then you know that I'm best at problem-solving when I'm distracted by other things. Other activities." She reached for the buttons of Beatrice's shirt and began undoing them. "Maybe we could revisit some happier memories, hm...?"

"A few favorites?" Beatrice gasped as Dorothy moved down to kiss and lick her neck.

"They're likely to keep me in this trance until morning." She straightened and kissed Beatrice hard. "No reason I can't enjoy the experience..."

Beatrice smiled. "None that I can think of."

Dorothy pulled Beatrice to her, and the fog closed around them.

CHAPTER EIGHT

DOROTHY HAD no way of knowing there actually *was* a reason she shouldn't enjoy the experience, or rather, a reason why tempering her enjoyment a bit would have been wise. As her mind raced with memories of Beatrice, her physical body remained slumped in the chair in her parlor. Her breath quickened, her cheeks flushed, and her fingers responded with tiny micromovements to the images created in her mind. And the Read twins, half-entranced but still harmonizing under their breath, inadvertently shared the passionate energy in a wave that quickly filled the room.

Myra and Susan, sleeping on the banquette curled in each other's arms, suddenly woke with a hunger for each other they couldn't explain. But they quietly rose and found a room where they could satisfy the urge without being observed. Myra gasped when Susan tore her undergarments in her haste, but a quick, "No it's okay don't stop," urged her eager hands onward. Susan stifled the first orgasm but slipping the side of her hand into Myra's mouth but, judging by how hard she bit down, decided she didn't care if they were overheard.

The other women sleeping in the room shifted and squirmed and rearranged their clothes without waking. They were suddenly assaulted by incredibly vivid dreams of naked flesh and sordid sounds. They licked their lips, and hands slipped under hastily loosened clothing. The women who were alert and standing guard also repositioned themselves, focused on their mission rather than the pheromones filling the air. Mouths went dry, and tongues swept across lips with almost inaudible gasps as they crossed and uncrossed their legs and tried to think of something, *anything* else.

And upstairs, directly above where Dorothy was currently being held prisoner, Violet didn't wake as she rolled across the mattress and settled on top of Trafalgar. Most of their clothing was gone and Violet's mouth was exploring the curve of her wife's breast when Trafalgar realized she was experiencing something more than a dream and opened her eyes.

"Vi, are you sure...? Your arm..."

"That's why I'm on top," Violet said.

Trafalgar had no reason to question that logic. She pressed her shoulders back against the pillow and looked up at the ceiling. This was not their house. Her pants and underwear were drawn down. The house was full of people. Violet's mouth was wet against the bend of her knee. If something happened, they would be required to leap into action. Violet's tongue began making shapes on her thigh.

Trafalgar put one hand in Violet's blonde curls and pushed her head down. Violet made a noise of surprise but eagerly accepted the repositioning. She draped one leg over Violet's shoulder and bit her bottom lip, closed her eyes, and moved her hips to compliment the movement of Violet's mouth.

Usually they were better at self-control than this. They were in the middle of a very intense situation, the expectation of privacy was exactly nil. But the idea of stopping, of postponing this ecstasy even a few hours, seemed impossible.

Trafalgar didn't last long. It felt like mere seconds before she pulled Violet's face to hers, kissed her wet lips, and gently positioned Violet to straddle her thigh. Violet pressed down against her and braced the hand of her uninjured arm against the headboard for leverage as she began thrusting. Her blouse hung open and Trafalgar could see the swaying breasts within. She leaned forward and nuzzled them, kissing until she found a nipple to suck.

The bed creaked and groaned beneath them, but Violet was doing her best to mask the sound with her own moans.

"Tell me your name," Violet gasped.

Trafalgar kissed her way past the freckles on Violet's upper chest to her neck. "My name is Trafalgar Rhys," she moaned, "and I am your wife."

"And I am yours."

Violet cried out and pulled Trafalgar's head to her, clinging to her as she rode out her orgasm, hips bucking before she finally relaxed. A moment later she went completely limp. Trafalgar went from the one being held to cradling the exhausted woman in her lap, lightly kissing her lips, cheeks, and fluttering eyelashes.

"What in the world was that?" Violet asked on an exhale.

"It was lovely," Trafalgar said. "That's the only name we have to give it right now."

"Mm-hmm." Violet's curls had fallen forward and veiled her eyes. Her smile was lazy and her head was a comfortable weight on Trafalgar's shoulder.

She definitely wanted to know what had prompted their lovemaking, but the light coming in through the window told her morning was about to break. And once the sun rose, they would have to figure out what to do about the Dorothy problem once and for all.

Dorothy didn't want to call it a dream. It was more real than that, more substantial. But as the Read twins relaxed their grip on her mind, the memory of what she had experienced began to flatten out and fade. She remembered Beatrice, the sound of a gasp in her ear and the pressure of fingers pressing down hard on her shoulders as they moved against each other. She regained consciousness with reluctance and fought to stay under even as she heard the house coming awake around her.

"...sorry if I crossed a line last night..."

"No, absolutely, it was-it was very nice..."

Dorothy struggled to stay under as long as possible. But Beatrice had already been taken back into the haze, and it felt like struggling only made the cloud darker.

"I hope you're not offended, but I-I saw what you were doing last night."

"I knew. I was glad you were watching."

Dorothy slowly raised her head, eyes squeezed shut, listening as the women around her continued their whispered conversations. Confessions? What exactly had happened in this room last night? She shifted in the seat and one of the Read twins tightened her grip on Dorothy's hand.

"She's waking up. Someone get Mrs. Rhys."

"I'm here," Trafalgar said. "Anything to report?"

Dorothy heard only an uncomfortable silence in response.

"All right," Trafalgar continued. "If everything is still on track, you're all dismissed. Go home, change clothes, get some rest. Thank you all for your help tonight."

Clothes rustled, footsteps sounded on the floorboards, and Dorothy heard a flurry of whispers as they filed out of the room.

Dorothy waited until the sounds of their exodus faded before she opened her eyes. The light was more than she expected and she turned away from the windows. She squinted and blinked back into focus before she faced forward.

Trafalgar stood in front of her, arms crossed over her chest. Her expression was neutral, but Dorothy could see pain and anger in her eyes. Violet was standing just behind her in an outfit Dorothy recognized from her own closet. In fact, she was pretty sure Trafalgar was also wearing a borrowed dress.

"Are you going to go quietly?" Trafalgar asked.

Dorothy pressed her lips together and tried to sit up straighter. "Yes. But with stipulations."

Trafalgar rolled her eyes. "You are in no position to~"

"Just hear me out. Please."

Violet whispered, "Trav. We owe her that."

"Nothing she can say will change my mind about the fact she needs help."

"Then there's no harm in listening to me," Dorothy said.

Violet made a sound between a cough and a chuckle. "She has a point."

Trafalgar worked her jaw. "Florence is upstairs, weak as a child, because of the trap you laid for her. Zilla Beverly is recuperating from several broken bones. The trauma you've inflicted on these women is immeasurable. I want you to know that before you attempt to sway me with some nonsense about time-travel."

"Would it make a difference if I told you I no longer believe time travel is the answer?"

Trafalgar arched an eyebrow. "You've been chasing this for six years. To say I'm skeptical that you've done a complete turn-around in a single night..."

"Call it divine intervention. The truth is, I have reason to believe I've overlooked something. There's another way, a better way, and I was too blind to see it. I can still find it, but it requires you to trust me.”

The veil dropped back over Trafalgar’s face. “Ah, here we are.”

“The answer is somewhere in the Inkwell’s library. I don’t know how long it will take to find. But I am willing to be a prisoner of the Society while I look. Constant guards. Chain me to the desk if it makes you feel better. Escorts from the library back to here for rest. You will always know where I am. I’ll never be out of your sight.”

“You ask for unlimited time to find an answer to your problem?”

“I *have* unlimited time!” Dorothy snapped, trying to pound her fist but only succeeded in rattling the chair against the floor. “I am immortal. I have life to...”

Words failed her. She looked away from Trafalgar and stared at a random point at the wall. It was there. The answer was there in her mind, and what she’d just said had almost made her trip over it. *I have life to spare...?* Was her alleged immortality the key to saving Beatrice?

“You made that argument last night,” Trafalgar said, when it seemed Dorothy wasn’t going to say anything else. “All you had to do was outlive us, and then you could do whatever you wanted. If you spent an entire night coming up with a tactic as common as feigning a surrender~”

“Two days.”

Trafalgar tilted her head to the side. “Pardon?”

“Give me two days in the library. If I don’t find what I’m seeking in that time, I will gladly go to whatever sanitarium you choose and sign myself in. No... I will allow one of you to do it. If I’m self-committed, I can leave whenever I want.”

She could see Trafalgar trying to figure out her angle. She turned to look at Violet, who shook her head and held up one hand.

“Two days. Under guard, escorted to and from the Inkwell.”

“And monitored here at all times,” Dorothy said. “There won’t be a minute of the day I’m not supervised. And it goes without saying you can take the artifact wherever you want. Hell, have Minty drop it in the middle of the Atlantic for all I care. I truly believe now that it isn’t the answer I was looking for.”

“And what is?”

“I don’t know!” Dorothy cried, her voice breaking. “That’s why I need the library. It’s there. I know it’s there. I just need to find the blasted thing.”

Violet whispered, “Trav...,” and nodded toward the hallway.

“Give us a moment to discuss.”

She followed Violet into the hall and stepped out of sight. Dorothy closed her eyes and took advantage of the silence to focus her thoughts. *I have life to spare.* She didn't even know if it was true. She hadn't seen many signs of ageing other than her gray hairs, but Trafalgar looked much the same as she did the day they'd met. Or maybe the changes were just so gradual that Dorothy couldn't see them... No, there was no sense in going down that road.

Whatever her subconscious was trying to point her toward, it required a belief that Riya Lennox was correct and she was immortal. That was the key.

Trafalgar came back with Violet. "We've come to a compromise. You will be allowed two days in the Inkwell's library under strict guard. Four society members will be upstairs with you at all times, and a member of the council will be present downstairs while you are in the building. When you adjourn for sleep or to eat~"

"I won't need to," Dorothy said quickly. "If I only have two days, I'll spend it all working~"

Trafalgar held up a hand. "You will not come back here. You will come to our home, where you will be our responsibility. If you require anything from this house, it can be brought to the Inkwell for you. At the end of two days, you will submit to being voluntarily committed to a facility of Cora's choice."

Dorothy nodded. "Understood. But if I do find what I'm looking for, the method we can use to save Beatrice, will you agree to hear me out?"

"Dorothy..."

"Please. At least hear my argument. I can't promise it will be better than the time-travel option, but I think it will be. I think it will be something we can all get behind."

Very softly, her voice almost inaudible, Violet said, "For Trix."

Trafalgar breathed in slowly and then nodded. "For Trix. I will hear you out. But I make no promises."

"Neither do I. I'm flying blind. But I'm confident."

Trafalgar's doubts were still written all over her face. She turned to Violet. "Watch her. I'll go inform Cora of the plan and make sure she's okay to be here alone with Florence."

Violet nodded and watched Trafalgar go up the stairs. As soon as she was gone, she walked into the room and stood in front of Dorothy.

"Thank you," Dorothy said. "I know you convinced her to give me a chance."

"You worked with her long enough to know I didn't convince her of anything. I just pointed out what she already knew. You're Lady Dorothy Boone. If you have even the germ of an idea, you won't let it go until you've exhausted all possibilities. It will be easier to keep hold of you if we let you exhaust whatever wild lark you woke up with."

Dorothy couldn't help but chuckle. "I'll take it."

Violet said, "Two days isn't a lot of time."

"It's enough," Dorothy said quietly. "It will be enough."

She could only hope she was right.

CHAPTER NINE

TWO DAYS. It was barely any time at all. It could be measured in hours, minutes. Hell, Dorothy could practically hear the seconds ticking by in her head as she was escorted to the Inkwell. Trafalgar had allowed her to take a bath and change into clean clothes before they left the house. Dorothy had used the preparation time to argue a case for starting the clock the moment she arrived in the library.

"Two days, from the moment I open the first book," she said.

"Two days from this morning."

"We need a definitive time, otherwise we'll end up arguing about the actual deadline."

Trafalgar had sighed and looked at her watch. "Noon."

It was a compromise, but one Dorothy could live with. She agreed.

Now she rushed up the stairs of the Inkwell, switched on the overhead lights, and looked at the rows of shelves in front of her. There were so many that, five years ago, they'd had to reinforce the floors to prevent everything from crashing down. No one had ever counted the books, and the only catalogue they had were half-hearted and incomplete lists the original owners had kept.

Why had she said two days? Yes, she had some twitch of an idea about where to begin, some itch scratching at the back of her subconscious, but she could have started with a month, two weeks, made them negotiate her down. But she'd said two days, and she was lucky to have it. She would just have to be creative.

She unbuttoned her sleeves and rolled them up as she approached the wall of books. She'd already exhausted most of the main texts in her original research. The big, heavy, obvious references were what had led her to time travel in the first place. It had to be something more obscure, something buried. That would at least give her a new starting place.

Her escorts had arrived and stood at the top of the stairs, two on either side, ensuring she wouldn't be able to get past them. She looked back and scanned their faces, realizing she only knew one of them by name.

"Is one of you Sadie? The speedy one?"

They looked at each other. Finally one raised her hand.

"Excellent. You can help me. I'm working against the clock. I can't tell you what I'm looking for, but if you can index some of these books, it will save me from scanning them all myself."

Sadie raised an eyebrow. "You want me to read all these books...?"

"Not read them. Skim. Get the gist of what they contain. And not the entire library. Just this section here."

"I'm supposed to be watching you..."

"In what world is there a chance I could get out of this room before you caught up and stopped me? It's the reason you're part of the guard in the first place. I just need a little help."

Sadie looked at the woman next to her, sighed, and relaxed her posture.

Dorothy pointed. "Start at that end, please."

"What am I looking for?"

"I don't know. Anything. It could be anything. Something about... life? Spare life? Bringing people back from the dead? I don't know. If I knew what to look for, I would narrow it down myself. Just look for anything to do with resurrection."

Sadie reached for a random book. When she pulled her arm back, Dorothy saw a tremor around her shoulder that quickly became a full-body blur. Dorothy watched the blur turn into a shimmer and looked away before she could get distracted by the spectacle. She stacked as many books in her arms as she could carry and went to the research desk. One book had already been placed there with several place-markers sticking out of the pages.

"What…"

One of the other guards said, "That's how Sadie works. Get used to it."

"Huh." Dorothy shook her head and put the book aside. The top book on her stack was a compendium of artifacts brought back to London by the Keepings. She took a deep breath, blew it out, and flipped the cover open to the table of contents.

She didn't bother to keep track of time. She knew other people were doing that for her, and knowing how much time she spent on each book would only make her panic and rush. She was able to dismiss books she'd never seen before. If the answer was in her head, it couldn't be something she had no knowledge of. She skimmed headers, glanced at drawings and diagrams, stared at maps, but nothing jumped out at her.

I have life to spare.

What could that possibly have triggered? The events in D'janira's cavern? No, that was the thinking which had led her to believe creating an alternate timeline was the only plan that would work. The Fountain of Youth? No… no, that wasn't it. But water. Yes! Yes, something to do with water.

Dorothy sat up straighter. "Water," she muttered.

One of the guards looked toward her, seemingly snapping out of a trance. "Ma'am?"

The light coming from outside was gone, and Dorothy realized with a start that she'd spent an entire afternoon going through the stacks of books on her table and letting her mind wander. How many hours had been lost? No matter. She couldn't think about that now, not when she had her hooks in something substantial.

"No, quiet…" She pressed her fingers to her temples and massaged in slow circles. She squeezed her eyes shut and focused. "Where's Sadie?"

She was answered by a gust of wind, and the woman was suddenly standing next to her again.

"Something to do with water." Dorothy grabbed one of the books Sadie had stacked on the corner of the desk. "Did you find anything that mentioned water, resurrection, the excess of… *quantitative life!* Life as a commodity!" She smacked the book cover with her palm. "Life to spare!" She looked up at Sadie, hopeful. "Anything along those lines?"

"No, nothing."

Dorothy pushed back her chair and went back into the stacks. "It's no bother, I think I know what I'm looking for now. Strode. Strode brought back a story about water. Not the fountain of youth, but something similar. And the cost of..." She suddenly turned. "Is Trafalgar here?"

"Downstairs, I think," one of the women said.

"Get her."

Dorothy went into the stacks. Abraham Strode's books. It was in something she'd read when they were first putting the library together. A curiosity more than anything else, a myth of a life-giving river. No, a waterfall? In a cave system... somewhere in the Middle East..."

She took down a book and flipped it open. It didn't look familiar so she dropped it on the floor and grabbed another. She had a pile of four books around her feet when Trafalgar appeared.

"Is this supposed to be evidence of a sound mind?"

"I fully admit I'm obsessed," Dorothy muttered. "I'm trying to remember something I saw in passing almost a decade ago. Or over a decade ago... it's been a very long time. I dismissed it immediately for some reason. But the knowledge is there..."

Trafalgar came forward, hesitant. "What are you looking for?"

"Water. There is a waterfall that can transfer life from one person to another. I dismissed it because of the *cost*. The cost was too high. Made it unfeasible. Restoring life costs life. You're effectively trading one life for another. Reviving a dead person by dying yourself."

"That is a heavy price..."

"Mm. Not for me."

Trafalgar sighed. "Dorothy. If you think we'll agree to let you sacrifice yourself for~"

"I'm immortal." Dorothy looked up from the book, raising her eyebrows as she stared at Trafalgar. "Impervious to ageing and illness. At least to a degree. Why not this?"

"Your immortality is theoretical at best. You can't prove it without actually ending your life. You have gray hair, Dorothy. Clearly there is some kind of ageing process going on."

Dorothy swiped her hand over her hair as if that would make the color disappear. "I can feel it. I know I'm right. I just need to find~"

A book dropped heavily into her hands, startling her.

Sadie appeared next to her like a developing photograph. First she was just a haze of color, and then she became a person.

"Page three-hundred and forty. I think that's what you're looking for."

Dorothy thumbed through the pages. Trafalgar stepped closer to read over her shoulder.

"This is it!" Dorothy said, excitedly jabbing the page with her finger. She read Strode's writing aloud. "A cavern in Thrace was said to contain a flowing river that passed through several rock faces. It was believed that a person who stood in a specific spot with the water washing over them could restore the life of someone placed in the runoff downstream. The location of this cavern of life is well-known by the locals but they warned heavily against actual use of it. The waters would drain the life of the donator... the donor, he meant... thus giving their life for that of their comrade."

"Draining the life of the donor," Trafalgar emphasized.

"The life of an *ordinary* donor," Dorothy said. "If I lost eighty, ninety, even a hundred years, it doesn't matter because I have an infinite supply."

Trafalgar closed her eyes. "Dorothy..."

Violet had joined them at some point, but Dorothy hadn't noticed her arrival until she spoke up. "The book also says a body is required," she said gently. "We don't have a body to restore life to."

Dorothy shook her head. "We'll figure it out on the way."

"On the way...?"

"To Thrace. Uh." She looked down at the book again. "Turkey. Modern-day Turkey."

Trafalgar and Violet looked at each other. "Not exactly the most stable region to visit right now. Let alone to go digging around in their ancient sites."

Dorothy spread her hand out over the open page. "Everything we need is right here. We can both get what we want. The timeline preserved and Beatrice alive again. One last mission. For old times' sake."

Violet saved Trafalgar from answering. "We need to discuss this first."

Dorothy tried to hold back her irritation. It was a reasonable request. She took a deep breath and nodded, closed the book, and held it against her chest.

"Of course. I await your judgment."

Violet only waited until she was at the foot of the stairs to give her verdict. "We need to let her go."

"Are you insane?"

"With an escort, obviously." Violet turned to face Trafalgar, arms crossed over her chest. "She's obsessed. She's absolutely convinced that there's a way to save Miss Sek. When the time travel plan was taken from her, she immediately locked onto another one. We have to let it play out or she'll come up with a new scheme, and God knows how that would play out. At least this way, you can have some control over the situation. And you can be there for her when it fails. I think following the idea to its natural conclusion will do more good than a full year in an institution. Maybe it will snap her out of it. Maybe it will make her finally accept the truth."

Trafalgar grimaced. Cora had been sitting in a booth when they came down, and she had slowly approached while Violet made her case. When she finished, she caught Trafalgar's eye and shrugged.

"She makes a good point, Trav."

"She does indeed." Trafalgar took a deep breath and then relaxed her shoulders. "A good point, and a correct one. I'll contact Minty and see if she's willing to take another run for us. Poor woman is probably sick of seeing our faces. We'll need to figure out who is going with her."

Violet and Cora looked at each other. "Well, that's obvious, don't you think?" Cora said.

Trafalgar raised an eyebrow.

"It has to be you, Trav," Cora clarified. "Just you, none of the rest of us."

"Absolutely not. That would be foolhardy, reckless, and completely insane. If I let my guard down for even a moment..."

Violet was already shaking her head. "She will only lash out if she's surrounded by jailers and guards. This has to feel like a normal commission. Just the two of you, like it used to be."

Cora said, "She's right. Dorothy will see you as an ally. Anyone else who goes with her would be seen as the enemy, even if it was me. She needs you, Trafalgar. And when this doesn't work, she's going to need you to keep from falling apart."

"You once told me you'd only ever had one name," Violet said with a small grin. "But that isn't true. For the Mnemosyne Society, and all us girls you saved from killing ourselves with our own powers, you were always Trafalgar and Boone."

Cora smiled. "One last mission. To say goodbye to Beatrice once and for all, and to save Dorothy from spiraling into grief and obsession."

Trafalgar sighed. "Well, we seem to have breezed right past the debate about whether the mission is even happening or not."

"Oh, it's happening," Violet said.

"Yes, yes." Trafalgar crossed her arms and looked toward the stairs. "Okay. But she may not want me anywhere near the mission. If that's a dealbreaker, then~"

Cora said, "Then I will volunteer, and I'll take a few of my ladies with me as a security force. But I don't think that's going to be necessary. She'll see that this is the way it has to be."

"Call Minty," Trafalgar said to Violet. "Ask her as politely as possible whether she would be available for a round trip to Turkey in the coming days. Make it clear we'll be willing to wait if she has more lucrative business lined up."

"We are?" Violet said.

"Not indefinitely," Trafalgar said, "but we're going to need time to prepare, just like any other mission. I want to know everything about this Thracian river before I allow Dorothy to storm into the caves and throw herself into the currents."

Cora said, "I'll see what I can find in my records."

"The entry Dorothy found was in one of Strode's books, so maybe anything he may have consulted with you about."

"Not a long list," Cora said.

Trafalgar motioned for Violet to follow her back upstairs.

Dorothy was sitting at the same table she'd been using for her research, fingers laced together on the table in front of her. She stood up quickly as soon as she saw them returning, and the women around her tensed as if preparing for a fight. Trafalgar waved them down and stood in front of Dorothy, the book-covered table between them. Dorothy perked up, eyes bright as she anticipated what their answer would be. Trafalgar held up one hand to stop any premature celebration.

"There remains the fact that according to the book, you require a body to resurrect. By your own account, there was no body left when Beatrice... vanished."

Dorothy smiled knowingly. "We won't need one."

Trafalgar raised an eyebrow, so Dorothy reached into the pocket of her coat and withdrew a handful of dirt. She held it out as if it was a prize.

"Dirt?" Trafalgar said.

"The same dirt which has been appearing in my pockets since Beatrice's disappearance. She's still here, Trafalgar. Just like she was present in the townhouse even though her physical body was comatose. You remember, she possessed the Dov and we were able to speak to each other. After she and the other elementals created the Void, my pockets started being filled with this dirt. It doesn't matter how often I empty them or wash my coats, there's always a handful of earth. She's giving me a sign that she's here. That she can be revived. Just like she said in my vision."

Trafalgar looked at Violet. Violet shrugged and nodded once.

"Very well," Trafalgar said. "We're going."

"We..." Dorothy cut her eyes toward Violet.

"As in you and me," Trafalgar said.

Dorothy raised her eyebrows. "Just like old times."

"No," Trafalgar said. "Not like them at all, really. But in honor of everything we've done for each other, and everything we've meant to each other, I owe it to you to see this through to the end."

She held her hand out across the table.

"One last adventure, Lady Boone?"

Dorothy smiled sadly and clasped Trafalgar's forearm. Trafalgar gripped Dorothy's arm in return.

"To the end of the road, Mrs. Rhys."

CHAPTER TEN

WHILE MOST of the *Skylarker* crew had homes around London, Araminta Crook and her command staff lived aboard the ship even when it was docked at the Rookery. Araminta had once explained it as simple economics; they spent so much time in the air and traveling to the Continent and back that it didn't make sense to pay for a flat in London that would remain empty for ten months out of the year. Dorothy knew the truth. The captain stayed on the ship simply because it was her home. She didn't need anywhere else because the *Skylarker* was her life.

The morning after Trafalgar agreed to go along with the Turkish mission, Dorothy asked for permission to go to the Rookery and make their travel arrangements. Florence, who had almost entirely recovered from her ordeal with Dorothy's trap, volunteered to escort her. Dorothy tried to apologize several times during the drive but Florence kept her eyes on the road and refused to acknowledge her presence, let alone her words. Eventually Dorothy took the hint and remained silent for the rest of the ride.

Not long before Dorothy was born, a debate had raged about whether Battersea Bridge should be replaced with a new bridge or something entirely new. Some official whose name she'd forgotten if she had ever known it, successfully debated that the bridge was too old to be repaired, obsolete due to other more modern and more popular bridges nearby, and a hazard due to its placement near a bend in the river. The time had come to look to the future. Airships were an incredibly new invention, still mostly in the planning stages, but there was enough scuttlebutt for financiers to believe it was the future of travel.

And so the Rookery was born. The main berths clung to either side of the Thames with a central bar extending over the water to connect the two halves. Dorothy found the *Skylarker* in the farthest berth on the northern shore. Florence followed her as far as the airship's open cargo hold and then stopped, giving her a bit of privacy.

Dorothy climbed the ramp but stopped before actually entering. "Ahoy-hoy," she called, then waited. A few minutes later, just as she was about to call again, Araminta emerged from deeper inside the ship. She hesitated when she saw her guest and then continued forward, smiling warily.

"Lady Boone. You know you don't need an invitation to come aboard."

"This is your home. And I'm afraid I've been mistreating it lately. It, and you. May I?"

"Of course." She looked past Dorothy. "Your friend can come too, if she'd like."

Dorothy looked back at Florence. "I think she's fine waiting out here. Just as long as I don't try to slip away while I'm aboard."

Araminta raised an eyebrow. "Have you been causing problems, Dorothy?"

"Always. But it seems this time the trouble has been hurting people I care about. It's something I'd like to make amends for, if you're willing to hear me out."

"Of course." She gestured for Dorothy to lead the way back into the ship. "Would my quarters be all right?"

"They would be perfect."

They remained silent as Dorothy led the way through the familiar corridors. The door to Araminta's quarters was propped open with a stack of books, which Araminta pushed out of the way with her foot. Dorothy went to the window and looked out. It was odd to see the docks and a stationary skyline across the water when she was so used to seeing clouds through these windows. She heard the door click shut behind her and decided she couldn't procrastinate any longer.

"Trafalgar said she only visited me at your urging. She said you were concerned for me."

"I'm sorry if I was overstepping the bounds of our friendship. But~"

Dorothy held up a hand. "I won't hear any sort of an apology from you. I had removed myself from the world, in more ways than one. You cared enough to wonder what that meant. And yes, your motives may have been less than kind, but your intentions... you were concerned. So thank you. It's good to know that I was missed."

Araminta nodded, uncertain about how to respond. "Honestly, Dorothy, I've been missing you even before you vanished last year. I've missed the person you used to be."

"Mm. About that. It's been brought to my attention, rather forcefully, that I've been acting like a complete bitch lately. Last night, I lay awake listening to women whispering outside my bedroom. They were stationed there as guards, in case I tried to escape. I was being held prisoner in my own home, a home which had just been attacked by people I considered friends." She leaned against the wall and crossed her arms over her chest. It was a classic defensive pose, but she didn't care that she was giving away her vulnerability. Not here. "It was eye-opening. I thought I was right. And... I don't know. Maybe I was able to see it because we'd found a new solution..."

"You were trying to save the woman you love, according to Trafalgar."

Dorothy looked at her. "She called you?"

"I called her. Last night. I wanted an update on your condition and she explained the whole situation. I think you know I'm sympathetic to that motive."

"Right. And that's another thing. I've been taking advantage of your gratitude for far too long."

"No~"

Dorothy held up a hand. "How much has your crew given up in commissions because you were flying me off on some lark? Your appreciation had no bounds, and I selfishly used it to my own advantage. I want to say, as of right now, your debt to me is paid. It was paid long ago. From now on, any flights I take with you will be as a paying customer."

She could tell Araminta wanted to argue, but stopped herself. "If you're absolutely certain."

"Absolutely," Dorothy said. "And as you said, now I have a unique understanding of what you went through when your wife was sick. Giving you extra time with her should have been a gift." Her voice broke and she looked away. "I should never have asked you to pay for a miracle like that."

Araminta crossed the space between them and hugged her. Dorothy tensed, then put her arms around the captain's waist and held her. Araminta was shorter than Dorothy, just barely above five feet, so her face pressed against Dorothy's collarbone.

"Well, there she is," Araminta said. "It's wonderful to have you back aboard, Dorothy. You've been missed terribly."

Dorothy chuckled and stepped out of the hug, turning away to wipe at her eyes. "Well. That makes this next question a bit easier to transition into..."

"You'd like to charter a trip?"

"Trafalgar told you?"

"It came up." She brushed her thumb across Dorothy's cheek to wipe away a tear. "One last free trip for old times' sake?"

"I fully intend to pay."

"And I fully intend to refuse it. I will take you wherever you need to go to get Beatrice back. After that, we can discuss a... an ally of the ship discount."

Dorothy smiled. "I suppose I can live with such an arrangement. If you insist."

"I do." She patted Dorothy's arm. "Thank you for coming here. For this conversation. I'm sure it wasn't easy for you. And I know the other conversation won't be easy, either."

"The other..."

"With Trafalgar. You owe her that much."

Dorothy pressed her lips together. "I was hoping we could... I don't know... leave it unsaid."

"No."

Dorothy started to argue, but realized it would be pointless. She rested her hands on Araminta's shoulders and nodded.

"I suppose you're right."

"I always am." Araminta leaned in and kissed Dorothy on the cheek. "Let me know when you need our services. We have a clear week ahead and should be ready to take you whenever you wish."

Dorothy nodded. "I don't deserve your friendship, Araminta."

"Not many do," the captain said with a wink. "That's what makes me so special."

Dorothy laughed.

The site in Strode's book wasn't actually Thracian but much further south in the Aydin Province of Turkey near Hisar. Trafalgar knew the area due to her research into the Temple of Apollo but she had never heard of the particular site Dorothy was so excited about. She found a map in the Society archives and took it home so she could plan their excursion. Strode had spent a month talking with the locals and trying to gain their trust so he could visit the site, but they refused his every request. Eventually he came home convinced the cave system existed but had no way of proving it.

"Perhaps it is for the best," Trafalgar read aloud from the notes. She had sensed Violet coming into the study behind her. "The site of the Thracian Resurrection Baths is clearly well-protected, and the good people of the world can rest easy knowing Kotys' temple will remain undisturbed and unexploited."

"Kotys," Violet said as she leaned against the edge of the desk next to Trafalgar's left arm. "Her followers were called, um, *baptes*, because their worship involved a bathing ritual."

"Very good, darling," Trafalgar said. "It certainly lends some credence to Dorothy's plan. Do you know anything else about her?"

Violet thought, and Trafalgar took the opportunity to admire her. She had taken off her blouse, leaving her in just a spaghetti-strapped undershirt. Her hair was pinned back to reveal the column of her neck. Trafalgar leaned back in her chair, ready to wait as long as necessary for her lover's wife to work.

"Oh! She's thought to be an aspect of Persephone."

"Spring and rebirth," Trafalgar said. "Interesting."

"Isn't it? Rebirth and a bathing ritual. It would be enough to convince me." She reached out and stroked the shell of Trafalgar's ear. "What about you?"

Trafalgar sighed. "If this was... before, if Dorothy and I were still partners, it would be enough for me to start packing a bag. But now I have to wonder if she's simply tilting at windmills again. She was fully convinced time travel was the right angle, to the point she spent quite a while in 1910. She sacrificed a full year of her life to that plan, and now she's just ready to abandon it for the next potential fix. If this fails, will she regress back to rewriting history? Will she come up with a third hair-brained option?" She sighed heavily. "Will her mind even be able to handle it if this fails?"

"It's a risk she'll have to take. More importantly, it's one she's willing to take." She looked away and then looked down at her hands. "I would like to make one request."

"Of course."

Violet stood and left the room. Trafalgar watched the door until she returned a few minutes later with something hidden in her hand. She took Trafalgar's hand, placed hers on top of it, and let a small but weighty item fall into her palm. When she removed her hand, Trafalgar saw a strange, wide ring which seemed to be made of brass. It was designed to be worn across two fingers; the second and third based on the width of the openings. There was a segment on the inside of the ring that seemed designed to be opened with the thumb. She pushed it now and saw a very small, very sharp needle.

"What's this?"

"Dorothy's plan requires a body. She doesn't seem like the sort to leave such an important detail up to fate. I don't want to make assumptions or imply devious intentions to someone you obviously care about. But I want your word that you will remain on your guard. If Dorothy gives you any reason to believe she intends to harm you..."

Trafalgar shook her head and stared at the ring. "I don't believe she would do anything so horrifying. Taking the life of one friend to save another. Even if we haven't been friends in a very long time. But I will take the precaution if it eases your concerns. Will this kill her?"

"I don't think so. But err on the side of caution. Don't use it unless you're willing to deal with that outcome."

"Understood." She carefully placed the ring in the pocket of her coat. "Cora called earlier. Dorothy is safely under guard once more at the townhouse, and our travel to Turkey has been arranged. As soon as we have a departure time, Captain Crook will fly us where we need to go. Now the only thing standing in our way is actually getting permission to land when we arrive."

"Things are still volatile there?"

Trafalgar sighed. "Last I heard, the military was bombing rebels at Mount Ararat. It's literally on the extreme opposite side of the country from where we need to land, but the rebellion is hardly an isolated incident. We still need to be extremely wary of who we interact with. Fortunately for us, the government is very forward-thinking when it comes to equality between the sexes. We're less likely to be turned away simply because we're women."

"So long as we contact the right people."

"Obviously." She checked her watch and pushed her chair back to stand. "Which is why I need to speak with Leonard Keeping."

Violet's face fell. "You're leaving? I thought we were in for the night."

"I'm sorry, love. But it's three hours later in Turkey, and I want to call them first thing in the morning so we can begin the process as quickly as possible."

Violet went to Trafalgar and straightened the collar of her blouse. "I suppose I understand. But you're about to leave for an unspecified amount of time with one of the only other people you've ever been intimate with. I'm not jealous but... I do admit a touch of preemptive withdrawal."

Trafalgar brushed her thumb over Violet's freckles. "Perhaps I can do something to alleviate a bit of your worry." She moved her hands to Violet's hips and walked her across the room. "The Keepings are still up to all hours. Dawn won't break in Ankara for a while yet. As long as I speak to Leonard before four o'clock, we shouldn't lose too much time. Tell me, love, what shall I do to put your mind at ease before I leave?"

Violet's shoulders touched the wall as Trafalgar bent down and began kissing her neck. Violet closed her eyes and reached for the waistband of her trousers. Trafalgar eased them down her hips and moved up to kiss her chin.

"Shall I get on my knees, Mrs. Rhys?"

"I would greatly appreciate it, Trav."

Trafalgar smiled, licked her lips, and knelt in front of her wife.

Dorothy's guards had given her a bit more trust by remaining on the second floor landing instead of stationing themselves right outside her door. Tonight it was Alice Nobbs and Albina Wallace, two of Cora's girls. She could still hear them talking, but it was easy to tune them out and pretend she was home alone. She had to pack for her mission. Possibly her final mission with the Mnemosyne Society, and almost certainly the last one she would take with Trafalgar. She hadn't realized how much she liked working with her. Even when they disagreed, maybe even especially when they disagreed, she'd never had as much faith in any of her previous partners.

"I have two options."

Dorothy jumped to the left, away from the voice that had materialized out of thin air next to her.

"One involves hurting the girls downstairs," Ivy continued. She was obviously used to people reacting to her this way. "I'm not sure where you stand on that, so I came up with a second option that just scuffs them up a little but without anything long-lasting."

"Where the hell have you been?" Dorothy asked.

"Around. Keeping an eye on things and waiting for an opportunity to move in. The Society seems to have lessened their presence today so now would be the best time to get you out of here."

Dorothy shook her head and continued packing. "I'm not going anywhere. Or more accurately, I'm working with the Society on a new plan."

"What? They were going to have you committed."

"And I convinced them to give me a chance. I don't need the artifact anymore."

Ivy said, "But I know where it is."

Dorothy paused with her hands in her wardrobe. "Pardon?"

"They sent that big girl away with it. Angel, I think her name is. I followed her. She took it to Threnody the Crafter."

Her original plan could be salvaged. She had all the information she needed about her targets, and now she knew where the artifact was. Ivy was her ticket out of the house.

"No," Dorothy said.

When Ivy spoke again, her voice was closer. "What do you mean 'no'? You told me earlier that you'd spent years figuring out this plan. Now with one more step between you and victory, you *refuse?*"

Dorothy snapped out of her brief fugue and went back to packing. "Our new plan has a better chance of success. It has Trafalgar's support. I'll be working with her, not against her. That's always been our secret weapon in the past. It may turn the tide this time as well."

Ivy grunted. "Just throwing away everything you've done so far... You believed in your plan. You believed so hard you were willing to turn your back on *everyone* and *everything* to make it happen."

"Because the plan involved changing the world so drastically that I had no idea what the future would look like afterward. For all I knew, my actions would erase everything and create a new world in its place. One without magic, one where events unfolded in a completely alien way. A blank slate for me to come back and... and correct some wrongs."

Ivy sighed. "Or maybe you're just afraid. If you went back in time and nothing changed, you wasted all that time. Maybe if you try this plan, you'll be equally unsuccessful. What then? Go for the artifact after all and try time traveling? At some point you have to give up, Dorothy."

"On the woman I love?" Dorothy said.

"People have given up on bigger things," Ivy said.

"Who?"

"Me." Ivy's voice was a low hiss, and Dorothy could tell she was crying. "I gave up on curing myself long ago. I'm never going to see my real face again. No one is ever going to look at me again. They might look at masks or makeup, but never me. You know the lengths I've gone to in order to end this curse, but I've made my peace with the fact that it's permanent. One day, unless I'm very fortunate, I'm going to die in the corner of some room and no one will notice until I start to smell."

Dorothy closed her eyes. "Ivy, I'm sorry..."

"Don't be. You've done more than anyone else to help me with this. Like I said, I'm resigned to the fact. No need to comfort me now. If I hadn't accepted it, I would still be running around and turning over every stone looking for a way to be normal instead of just living the best life possible given the circumstances. You've spent all this time trying to find an answer. Trix wouldn't expect you to throw your whole life away for what's starting to look like a lost cause."

There was a knock on the bedroom door. "Lady Boone? Are you talking to someone?"

Dorothy hesitated for only a second. "Yes, Alice. I'm speaking with Ivy Sever. She came here with the intention to help me sneak out, but I've told her that I have no intention of escaping."

Silence from the other side of the door. Finally Alice said, "Oh."

"I'm hoping you will appreciate my honesty in this matter. I could have lied, but I don't want any hint of deception between me and the rest of the Society."

"Sure. Okay. Um. I-I'm not sure what we should do about Miss Sever, to be honest, ma'am. Mrs. Rhys and Miss Hyde didn't give us any guidelines if she was to show her fa~ uh, c-come back."

Dorothy looked at the last place she'd heard Ivy's voice. "She'll remain here until they return, and then they can decide what to do with her."

"I'm not agreeing to that," Ivy said under her breath.

"Do you believe that will be acceptable, Alice?"

More silence. "I suppose so. I... I think she should stay in there with you. The door stays closed until Trafalgar or Cora comes back."

"Fair enough."

Ivy snorted.

"Ivy agrees to the terms."

"Well. Okay, then."

She heard footsteps on the stairs. "You have to face the consequences of your actions earlier."

"I only did those things because *you* told me to."

"I'll bear my portion of the blame," Dorothy promised. "But I have hope that we can all mend the rifts between us. Perhaps even if this mission is a failure, we can at least claim that victory."

The bed sagged under Ivy's weight as she threw herself down onto it. Dorothy started to protest but decided it wasn't a battle worth fighting.

She had a trip to prepare for.

CHAPTER ELEVEN

TRAFALGAR DIDN'T bother knocking when she arrived at the home of Agnes and Leonard Keeping. The downstairs had been transformed into a base of operations. The rest of the Society referred to it as the Keeping Conglomerate. The former Elephants the couple had taken in seven years ago had been tutored in every discipline the older pair had spent their lives mastering. The girls were now adept in myriad hand-to-hand fighting styles, expert sharpshooters, champion-level fencers, and so well trained in etiquette that any of them could crash an elite party without causing a stir.

All the lights were on in the main room, but Trafalgar only saw three women stationed at their desks. Emily Tripp was the closest to the door and rose to greet her.

"How are Isabella and Zilla?" Trafalgar asked.

"We just heard that they're both improving," Emily said. "They might have to take a little time away, but we'll pick up the slack in the meantime."

Trafalgar nodded. "Excellent news." She glanced toward the stairs. "I know it's quite late, but I was hoping I could steal some time with them."

Emily said, "Agnes hasn't had a normal sleep schedule for a while now. Naps all around the clock, usually, so if she's not up now, she will be soon. I can go check."

"Thank you. I only need her to make a phone call. Nothing too strenuous."

"I'll let her know."

Emily headed upstairs and Trafalgar ventured into the main office. The other women currently at work, Helena and Mabel, looked at her with infuriatingly knowing smiles.

"Hello, Mrs. Rhys," Mabel said.

Trafalgar rolled her eyes in mock exasperation. She should have been prepared for the ribbing. "Oh lord..."

"How is the wife, Mrs. Rhys?" Helena said, linking her fingers together under her chin. "Are you taking good care of our Violet?"

Trafalgar blew air out through her lips. "How long will this teasing persist?"

"Until you stop being annoyed by it!" Mabel said, so chipper it would've been annoying if she wasn't so adorable.

Helena said, "We're just being nosy. We all loved Violet when she was staying with us. She's the first of us to really blossom."

"Blossom?" Trafalgar said.

Helena's cheeks flushed. "I didn't mean... I didn't think about the flower metaphor. But you know. She has a real profession now. She's married. We all love working with the Keepings, don't get me wrong, but Violet is who we all aspire to be."

Trafalgar smiled. "It's not a bad goal, honestly. She's quite impressive."

Mabel giggled and hunched her shoulders. "So she's still happy?"

Trafalgar pictured how she had left Violet; sprawled on their mattress, nude from the waist down, cheeks flushed and a goofy smile pasted on her face. "Oh yes, I can assure you she's quite happy."

Emily returned at that moment, saving her from any further questions or teasing. "She's in the library and would be more than happy to see you."

"Thank you very much." To the women in the office, Trafalgar said, "We'll speak again later, I'm sure."

The sound of their laughter followed her upstairs. Emily had left the library door open but Trafalgar rapped her knuckles against the doorframe before she stepped inside. The only light came from the desk lamp, which created looming shadows on the shelves and deepened the corners. Trafalgar was so comfortable in the house, and the Keepings were such lovely people, that the resulting impression was coziness rather than fear.

Agnes Keeping finished what she was writing, took off her glasses, and sat up straighter. Trafalgar didn't know exactly how old she or Leonard were, but they were without question the oldest members of the Society. They might have been the oldest people she'd ever known. Despite that, and despite the fact she looked thinner than the last time they'd spoken, the spark in her eyes hadn't dimmed a bit. She smiled as brightly as ever and folded her hands in front of her.

"Trav. Wonderful to see you again."

"And you." Trafalgar nodded at the pages. "Finally working on your memoirs?"

Agnes scoffed. "No, not quite yet. This is just a crossword. Tires my mind out. Helps me get to sleep. Is Violet well?"

"She's fantastic. She sends her love." Agnes had given Violet away at the wedding and, later, Violet cried when she said the Keepings were the closest thing to parents she'd ever known. "She would have come herself, but she knows that if she ever sets foot inside this house you won't let her leave again. At least not until you've gotten a full rundown of everything that's happened in her life since the last time you saw her."

"A wise girl, that one."

"How is Leonard?" She tried to keep the concern out of her voice.

Agnes sighed and shook her head. "Poor man. He's not in pain, but it's clear that... well." She waved a hand. "We've both agreed that when the quality of life reaches a certain nadir, we will do the proper thing for each other. Bastard is just making sure I'm the one who has to do the difficult thing." She raised an eyebrow and then swiped her hand through the air. "But you didn't call on me in the middle of the night to discuss such morbid things."

"No..." She did, however, put a pin in it to return to the subject later. "I need your assistance in arranging a visit to Turkey. The western coast, near Hisar."

"Shouldn't be too difficult." She looked at her watch. "Very early there. Rami will be available." She opened one of the desk drawers and began digging. "I assume this is some sort of treasure hunt for you and Violet?"

Trafalgar said, "Treasure hunt, of sorts. But for me and Lady Boone."

Agnes looked up, eyebrows raised. "I thought that was as dead and buried as anything the Society explores."

"It is," Trafalgar said. "Violet is the only partner I require, in every sense of the word. But this is something that we have to do together. One last adventure."

Agnes made a quiet sound as she withdrew a book and began thumbing through it.

"What?"

"Nothing, dear."

Trafalgar sighed and raised her eyes to the ceiling. "Agnes, we're practically family. Whatever you have to say, even if it's tough love, I will take it in the spirit you intend."

Agnes rested her hand flat on the open page. "I knew Dorothy before the two of you started working together. And I was aware of you from your reputation. You were both incredibly good at your chosen professions, but neither of you would ever be great because you spent half of your energy on a ridiculous rivalry. Once you teamed up, you were able to focus on the work."

"And look where it got us," Trafalgar said. "A plague running amok in London and a flood of magic that could have destroyed the world."

"Not to mention those girls downstairs, who you were instrumental in rescuing and rehabilitating. The Mnemosyne Society itself owes its very existence to you! Dorothy's temporal-slipping acquaintance proved the group survives well into the future, for better or worse. I am confident that the work we've done will continue long after Leonard and I pass on. I'm certain Abe Strode would have taken some comfort in it as well. My point is, the two of you are stronger together. Don't call this the end until you're absolutely certain."

Trafalgar said, "I'm quite happy with the work I'm doing with my wife, thank you."

"And it's very good work. And Dorothy..." Agnes sighed and shook her head. "I can't judge her work because there really hasn't been any since Beatrice died. She's consumed by trying to find answers that I don't believe exist..." She narrowed her eyes. "Is that what this is about? Another fool's errand to find a woman who has been gone for seven years?"

"It's the final attempt. Dorothy and I came to an agreement. If this doesn't bear fruit, she will give up the chase and submit herself for treatment. We're humoring her."

"You may think you're humoring her," Agnes said, going back to flipping pages, "but she no doubt believes she's just using you. Be careful the lines don't blur."

"I shall remain vigilant."

"Mm." She tapped the page and reached for her telephone. "Rami is a good man. He'll take care of you even if things get heated up in the area."

"Is there much potential for heat?"

Agnes wrinkled her nose and made a so-so motion with her free hand. "Hello, Rami. I do hope I'm not calling too early... No, you're right, it is much earlier here, but not everyone is as stalwart as I am." She laughed. "Excellent. Unfortunately I'm not calling for myself but for a very dear friend. We're hoping you can work your magic for them to pay your country a visit."

Agnes listened. Trafalgar held up her crossed fingers. After a moment, Agnes' smile widened.

"Wonderful news, Rami. Let's work out the details now while we're all sitting here."

Dorothy didn't remember falling asleep until she was suddenly awakened by a commotion downstairs. She felt the body next to her, knew her head was resting on someone's shoulder, but all she could see was a cratered pillow and rumpled sheets. She lifted her head and blinked her eyes back into focus as she tried to make sense of it. Her memory finally caught up with her as Ivy broke her silence.

"You fell asleep, and I didn't want to wake you up."

"Very considerate of you." She sat up and pushed her hair out of her face. People were speaking in raised voices on the ground floor, but she couldn't make out what was being said. "Any idea what's happening down there?"

"Not a clue. Everything was quiet and then suddenly, this."

Dorothy slipped off the edge of the bed and went to the door. Mary Waterson was on the landing, turned to look down the stairs with one hand on the newel post. She whipped around when she heard the bedroom door open, but Dorothy held her hand up for a truce.

"Whatever is happening downstairs, I had nothing to do with it."

"Edith Bowles just showed up in the parlor using one of those portals Janya can apparently make now. She's got one of her golems with her."

Dorothy's face became hot. She stepped out of her room and closed the door behind her. Mary turned to face her fully.

"You're not supposed to leave the room."

"I know, but I worry Cecil might be trying to be... I don't know. Valiant, maybe. I need to let him know I don't require rescuing. Let me go down there and talk to them before this situation spins entirely out of control."

Mary pressed her lips together, a line appearing between her eyebrows.

"I swear, I won't leave the house. Look, I'm in my stockings. I would allow you to escort me down, but you must stay here because there's an invisible assassin in my bedroom and you must make sure she stays there."

"An invisible--"

Dorothy winced. "I realize it sounds like the most pathetic ruse I could have come up with..." Something crashed downstairs. "Please, I can de-escalate the situation but I must go down there now."

Mary hesitated another second, during which someone in the kitchen shouted, "Remove your hand!" Mary sighed and motioned for Dorothy to go.

Dorothy hurried down the stairs as fast as she could without risking injury. She pivoted and ran into the parlor where Angel had one meaty hand closed around Edith's neck, and Honour Battle was holding a golem at bay with a pistol aimed at its featureless head. The four combatants were surrounded by a ring of women who were obviously unsure what to do.

"Everyone stop this instant!" Dorothy shouted. The tension in the room snapped like a rubber band. Every head spun toward her, save for the golem's. "Edith, if your arrival here was a misguided attempt to liberate me, it's completely unnecessary."

Edith grunted and swatted at Angel's hand. Angel looked to Susan McAlister for confirmation, then let her go. Edith exhaled roughly and rubbed her throat, glaring at the bigger woman as she coughed to get the roughness out of her voice before she spoke.

"I'm not here to break you out. Word's spread about your plan. The miracle water thing."

Dorothy said, "How? No one knows about that except..." She sighed. "My guards, I suppose. Do you have insight to share?"

"Not as such. Don't know anything about it. Sadie mentioned you need a body to do the resurrecting. Beatrice didn't leave one of them behind. But I can make bodies." She hooked her thumb toward the golem, which was still lurking behind Honour. Dorothy hadn't noticed before, but it did seem to be the same size and shape as an average woman. "This one is fair dumb," Edith explained. "Just barely animated. It'll go where you tell it, sit and stand, walk or run, whatever, but nothing much more complicated than that. I figure you can take it with you, just in case you need something for the magic to work."

Angel relaxed and looked at the golem. "She didn't tell us none of that..."

"You didn't give me a chance!"

"You walk through that portal with one of them things stomping in behind you like some kind of bareknuckle brawler~"

"It's not even taller than Susannah!"

"We've all seen what them things are capable of!"

Dorothy whistled shrilly. "Enough! We're all going to chalk this up to a misunderstanding. No hurt feelings, no repercussions. All right? Edith, you could have found a more diplomatic way to make your arrival. Angel, you may have jumped the gun. Everyone is to blame, to some degree. Are we okay with that?" Murmurs of agreement. "Very well. Edith... thank you. The golem may indeed come in very useful in our mission."

"I'll let Cecil know. It was his idea."

"Ah. Well, send him my appreciation. If that's all...? I'll be upstairs."

Dorothy turned and was startled to see Cora was standing a few steps behind her. Cora looked exhausted. Her hair hung loose, the streaks of gray more pronounced than when she wore an up-do, and she was dressed in an undershirt and trousers. Her arms were crossed over her chest. They stared at each other silently for a moment, all the women in the parlor behind Dorothy observing in silence as well. She knew most of them probably thought they were about to see another fight.

"It was a lovely speech, Dorothy."

"I... um. Thank you."

Cora finally smiled, her whole body relaxing. "I think I recognized you for the first time in a couple of years just now. Lovely to see you again, old friend."

Dorothy smiled ruefully. "It felt good, to be honest."

"Mm-hmm." Cora dropped her arms and turned to go back into the kitchen. "You're going back upstairs, right?"

"I was on my way."

"Good."

Dorothy watched Cora until she disappeared into the kitchen. She looked back into the parlor, where all the women suddenly found something else to give their attention. Dorothy smoothed her hands over her hair and ascended the stairs to return to her cell. She had a big trip coming up and she could use all the rest she could get.

CHAPTER TWELVE

THE MORNING sun hit the Thames and reflected up onto the underside of the *Skylarker*, creating golden shimmers across the underside of its envelope and gondola. The crew was loading their final provisions for the journey, carrying large boxes from the docks into the ship. Edith had escorted the golem to the *Skylarker* the night before and it was now sitting on a crate in the cargo hold for lack of anywhere else to put it. Trafalgar saw that the crew were mostly ignoring the being's presence but still taking wide paths to avoid getting to close to it.

Araminta was on the gangplank with the harbormaster when Dorothy and Trafalgar approached. Violet was with them, having volunteered to carry Trafalgar's valise so she could see them off. Trafalgar knew that the reason was also, at least partially, to prove that she was still capable of doing things despite her gunshot wound. It was continuing to heal and looked like it was weeks along, but Trafalgar was still distrustful of quick fixes and was grateful to see Violet wasn't struggling with the bag.

The harbormaster left just before Dorothy reached the ship.

"Everything in order?" Trafalgar asked.

Araminta nodded. "Just making sure the berth will still be ours when we get back. Lots of ships vying for a spot." She clapped her hands together. "Are we ready?"

"Indeed we are," Trafalgar said. "And thank you once again, Captain Crook, for always being there when we need you."

"I don't do this for just anybody, you know," Araminta said. "You two have always been my favorite passengers."

"Even with the danger to which we've exposed your crew?" Trafalgar asked.

Araminta smiled. "Because of it, Mrs. Rhys." She winked and walked up the gangplank to the tannoy control. "Thabisa, set your course and take us out as soon as we've pulled up stakes."

The navigator responded with a brief, "Aye, captain, setting course."

Araminta used both arms to motion Dorothy and Trafalgar inside. "Say goodbye to the land, ladies, because we're not going to see it again for the better part of the day."

Trafalgar stepped to one side to say goodbye to Violet, kissing the corner of her mouth due to the fact they were in public. Their fingers brushed as Violet handed over the valise.

"I'll see you on the weekend, my love," Trafalgar whispered.

"Be safe," Violet said. Trafalgar could see the fear in her eyes. She'd heard too many second-hand stories of these missions to ignore the dangers they might encounter.

Trafalgar adjusted the collar of Violet's gown, an acceptable public display of their love. "We've always come back before."

"Didn't Lady Boone technically die on two different occasions when you were partners?"

"I probably exaggerated those stories. All of our missions were quite dull, to be honest. Would have bored you to tears if I stuck to the truth."

Violet raised an eyebrow. "Oh, is that so?"

"Mm-hmm. Hours upon hours spent in dusty libraries. I once suffered a very bad papercut."

"Such hazards. Which finger?" Trafalgar held up her forefinger and Violet kissed it. "How miraculous there's no scar."

"I was very lucky. And so were you. Don't forget that." She put her hand over the spot where she knew the bullet had gone on. "If you feel any weakness, anything odd at all—"

Violet nodded. "Immediately to the doctor. Yes, love, I know." She kissed Trafalgar again. "I will spend the time you're gone sleeping and recuperating the old fashioned way. You have my word."

"That's all I ask." She noticed Dorothy lingering nearby, clearly eager to get underway but reluctant to interrupt. "I should probably go. I love you."

"I love you," Violet said at the same time. "Go. And be safe in libraries."

"Always."

They parted, and Trafalgar followed Dorothy up the gangplank. Araminta waited until they were clear and pressed the button to close the gate and prepare for launch.

The ship drifted out from its berth ten minutes later, turned slowly to line up with the river, and began its slow sail out toward the coast.

Dorothy and Trafalgar had both woken early that morning to make the departure so, as the ship followed the Thames out of England, they settled into their respective quarters for a quick nap. Dorothy woke and looked out the porthole to see they had already reached the Continental coast. She checked her watch, grateful to see they were making excellent time, and left her room to attend breakfast with the crew. It was her way of making amends for all the invitations she'd turned down during her previous trips aboard the ship. She understood now that her obsession had caused her to act cruel and dismissive to people who were going out of their way to do her a favor. They were her *friends*, and she'd treated them like servants. It was unforgivable, but she hoped they would take pity on her.

Trafalgar pored over the research Strode had done on the "Thracian Resurrection Baths" as the *Skylarker* skimmed the border of France and Germany. The area was full of myths and legends about people who had used the baths in times of war. Generals who sacrificed themselves for a great soldier, lovers making the ultimate sacrifice for a soulmate, and several cases of parents who gave their lives to bring back a child.

Every story indicated the returned person was fully revived and in robust health, but there were no long-term reports. She hadn't expected follow-ups, given how long ago the stories allegedly happened, but it left her with so many questions. Did they live out the rest of their lives as normal? If they died of a disease, were they still afflicted when they came back or did resurrection also provide healing? And what of the golem? It lacked features, it had no distinct body shape. If Beatrice did possess the creature, would she look like that forever? Or would her soul manipulate the material in some way to make it look like herself?

The stories were all over a thousand years old. The area had seen a lot of turmoil, to the point where the location was off by over four hundred kilometers. Their plan called for three days in Turkey but she was starting to worry that, even with Rami's help, it wouldn't be enough time to dig through the errors and miscommunications and actually find the Baths.

As the airship was rocked by mild turbulence over the Alps, Dorothy stayed on the viewing deck and stared down at the mountains. She was going to honor the promise she made to Trafalgar, no matter what happened. She had gotten enough distance to see how far over the line she'd gone, and she was grateful Trafalgar still cared for her enough to give her this much rope. If they failed, that was it.

The end of this trip would be the end of it all, one way or another. She didn't know if that meant she would retire, resign her position with the Society, or if there would be a way to earn back her place. She had a feeling that her decision would depend on whether or not they came back with Beatrice. Without her, and without the purpose of saving her, she didn't think she wanted any part in the mysteries of the world.

If this was how her career ended, she would have to spend the rest of her potentially very long life dealing with the fear that she'd done much more harm to the world than good.

She was still considering that when Araminta found her after lunch. The captain's eyes were warm, but her smile was guarded. She took a seat on the other side of the L-shaped banquette from Dorothy.

"We seem to be making good time," Dorothy said.

"The winds and weather have been kind to us, yeah. We radioed ahead to let them know we might be landing a little earlier than we thought."

"Wonderful. I hope you're not pushing your crew too hard."

Araminta smiled. "If I didn't push them hard, they would assume I'd been replaced by an imposter. I'd be facing a mutiny."

Dorothy sighed. "Well, I appreciate it. But I don't think I deserve it."

"The crew loves you as much as I do," Araminta said.

"Really?" Dorothy raised an eyebrow. "Given the way I treated them the past few years? This ship? *You?* I'm surprised I'm not being shunned everywhere I turn."

Araminta sighed, stood, and moved to sit next to Dorothy. They were both facing the windows now, and Araminta put her arm across Dorothy's shoulders.

"Do you realize who you're talking to? I became a bit of a tyrant after Miranda's illness. I took all my pain and sorrow and worry and I turned it into anger. I was a very strict and unforgiving captain. Luckily the crew understood why I was taking it out on them, and they didn't throw me into the English Channel. After she passed away, I changed again. I don't think I spoke to anyone outside of flight-related business for... weeks. Even though you pulled off your miracle, it didn't change the fact she was gone."

Dorothy sighed and looked down at her hands.

"I'm not saying Beatrice is dead. I don't know what to believe about the situation, honestly. But I know she hasn't been with you for a very long time. So that's a kind of grief. It's a loss, and it's pain that you must cope with. You haven't been coping very well. You shut yourself off, ignored your friends, let the world move on while you dug in your heels on a single problem. A worthy problem, to be sure, but you stepped out of life. The rest of us kept going."

Dorothy kept her head down. Her voice was quiet. "I'm trying to come back. Whatever happens here, I want to come back."

"I know. And if there's anyone who knows what you're going through, it's me. The loss becomes everything in your line of sight. But eventually you'll wake up and see everything you still have. And you're going to want to grab at it with both hands."

"Thank you, Minty." She sighed and looked at her hands. "Look at the state of me. I've never had fingernails this long in my life. I usually trim them down before going off on an expedition."

Araminta took one of Dorothy's hands and brushed her finger over one of the nails. "It's not so bad. Though if you succeed and bring Beatrice back, you might want to take care of them before your grand reunion." She winked.

Dorothy chuckled and bumped her arm against Araminta's.

"Be strong, Lady Boone. It isn't a short road by any means, but you don't have to travel it alone."

"I'm striving to remember that."

They sat together in silence and turned their attention to the window to watch as the airship made its final approach.

CHAPTER THIRTEEN

ABRAHAM STRODE'S first exploration of the ruins around Hisar occurred in 1908 with a group of German archaeologists. They contributed to uncovering the Temple of Apollo and naturally set off a wildfire of further excavations of the surrounding area. Their destination was about thirty kilometers further north in the Beşparmak Mountains. Dorothy and Trafalgar both went to the viewing deck to get a look as the *Skylarker* arrived in Turkey.

"Not far now," Trafalgar said.

Dorothy looked at her. "I intend to hold up my end of the bargain. No matter what happens here, success or failure. I know it's my last resort."

"Even though the time traveling artifact remains a possibility?"

"Time travel..." Dorothy blew out hard and leaned forward the rest her elbows on the railing. "I've given this a lot of thought during my recent isolation. I was so certain that I could fix everything by removing magic from the equation. I could see it in my mind's eye, like switching tracks for a train. But with the benefit of hindsight, I see that I was ignoring so many variables... I only saw the things that benefited my goal. If you hadn't been at the townhouse when I returned, if I'd gone through with it, I would have been the greatest threat London, or the world, has ever known."

Trafalgar shrugged. "I don't know. The benefit of changing

history is that none of us would be aware of the change. We could be living in an altered world right now without being aware of it."

"Perhaps." She tilted her head back and looked at the sky. "I think I prefer this world. Even with all its darkness and loss and all the grief. Even if it's a world without Beatrice Sek, it's a world where the Beatrice I know and loved existed. If only for a brief time. How could I ever have endangered that?"

"I couldn't have said it better myself."

A tone sounded, and the all-ship tannoy system sparked to life with a burst of static. "This is your captain speaking. We are minutes from landing, so if everyone would kindly take a seat in the interest of safety, I would be greatly obliged."

They went to the banquette and fastened the harnesses across their waist as the ship descended into the city's hangar.

When they were safely docked, they headed down to the cargo hold and unstrapped the golem from its safety restraints. As they were maneuvering it toward the lowered gangplank, a dark-haired young man with a trimmed goatee approached and waited at the base of the ramp. He looked to be twenty, maybe a few years beyond that, and bursting with enthusiasm. He smiled when he caught Dorothy's eye and raised a hand in greeting.

"You are Agnes and Leonard's friends, I assume? Rhys and Boone?"

"N~" Dorothy caught herself before she corrected him. It was still bizarre to hear Trafalgar referred to as anything else. "Indeed we are," she said. "You would be Rami Demirel?"

His smile widened as he relaxed his posture. "Yes. You must call me Rami. Any friends of the Keepings, after all. A magnificent couple. I hope they're doing well."

Dorothy flinched. "As well as can be expected, I think."

Rami nodded thoughtfully. "I must get to London soon to visit them while I still have a chance. It seems unlikely they will be making the journey here again."

Trafalgar said, "That would be wise."

"Hm," Rami said softly, then shook his head and refocused. "Anyway, talk for another time. For now we have a long drive ahead of us. Your chariot awaits, ladies." He looked at the golem. "I was told to have space for an unusual passenger, but I didn't quite envision this."

"Can your vehicle accommodate it?" Dorothy asked

"Absolutely. It's an… it?"

Dorothy said, "It's a complicated explanation so for now, yes."

"I suppose that is all I can ask. Would you like me to carry any of your bags?"

"We brought very little," Dorothy said, pulling the strap of her bag up onto her arm. Trafalgar had her own valise, which had more books than clothes. Dorothy understood their schedule allowed them three days in Turkey, but she also knew they both believed they would have their answers within twenty-four hours. One way or another, this was going to end very soon. She tried not to get her hopes up, even though the bag currently digging into her shoulder contained a dress shirt, slacks, underwear, and shoes in Beatrice's size.

"If all is ready," Rami said, "then let us get on the road before we lose too much of the day. It's quiet right now, but it's difficult to say just how long that will last."

"Story of our lives," Trafalgar mumbled.

"Do you need help with your bags?" he asked.

"We're fine," Dorothy said.

He nodded, clapped his hands, and motioned for them to follow him out of the hangar.

Rami's vehicle was a Chevrolet Capitol, a shining black truck with tall wooden panels on either side of the bed. The golem climbed into the back without being prompted, sitting with its back against the tall cabin. There was space on either side of the creature for their bags, so Dorothy packed them in and guided its hands down to hold them in place. Rami didn't look particularly confident about the safety of the creature, but Dorothy knew from experience that Edith's creations could withstand a great deal of punishment without permanent damage.

Trafalgar took the center of the bench seat next to Rami, and Dorothy sat next to the passenger door. She had brought a wide-brimmed hat and goggles but was still worried about how long the sun would be beating down on the side of her face during the drive. She regretted cutting off so much of her hair, which could have acted as a natural curtain. But if she got through this ordeal with that as her biggest regret, she would consider it a win.

The road into the mountains was smoother than she expected. Rami waited until they were past the edge of town before he broke the silence.

"Agnes and Leonard were a dream to me when I was a kid. Ten, fifteen years ago, we'd get word that they were coming, and my friends and I would go running to be there when their ship arrived at the harbor. They would hire three or four of us to be their gofers. We would run to get them food, water, sundries, all sorts of things, anything they needed. And they paid handsomely, too! Their generosity is how I got this truck. I bought it so I would always be their first choice when they came. Then they started recommending me to their friends!" He laughed and smacked the steering wheel. "Most lucrative, and a very good investment, don't you think?"

"Quite savvy," Trafalgar agreed.

"Worked out very well for me. So much work now *I* hire my friends when there's too much work to be done." He sighed. "Definitely a good purchase. Amazing what one truck can do, eh?"

"Absolutely."

A sandstorm blew across the road ahead of them, and Rami steered with one hand as he cranked up the window with the other. Dorothy did the same with her window.

"Is your, um..." He twisted to look out the back window. "Is that going to be okay?"

"We honestly don't know," Dorothy admitted. "But we assume it can handle most anything that gets thrown at it."

Rami nodded and then shook his head in disbelief. "Some of the things you and the Keepings and all your friends get up to. It's amazing. And seeing it firsthand is almost payment enough for me." He looked at them and quickly added, "Almost payment enough."

Trafalgar smiled. "You will be compensated for your time. Any spectacle can be considered a bonus."

Rami returned her smile and nodded his approval.

The mountains loomed on the horizon and quickly grew to fill the windscreen. Rami slowed and Trafalgar unfolded a map on the dashboard that he could reference without taking his eyes off the road. Strode and his earlier expedition had marked their route well, but they'd also used unofficial roads which might not have survived the intervening decades. Fortunately Dorothy was a stalwart navigator and spotted the turnoff before he passed it.

They squeezed between two mountains on a rutted one-lane road, the ground rising up on either side of the truck. Dorothy felt a bit of claustrophobia on the tighter passes, well aware that it would be difficult to open the doors if that became necessary. The elevation also meant that they were pressed back against the thin cushion of the seat. She could feel the metal frame against her shoulders. It felt like she was on a platform being pulled up into the sky inch by slow inch.

She looked over her shoulder to check the golem, but it didn't seem affected by the treacherous road. She watched it shift position and brace itself against one side-wall with its foot. How much intelligence did the creature actually have, she wondered. Just the act of moving its foot so it wouldn't fall suggested some kind of sentience. But was it just a physical reaction or was there some kind of thought process behind it?

"Almost there," Rami said. "Just around this bend, I think."

"Wonderful," Trafalgar said, sounding as unsettled as Dorothy felt.

As predicted, it was only a handful of minutes before the road leveled out and Rami took them around a stone outcropping to reveal what looked like the edge of a crater. When he stopped the truck and they climbed out, Dorothy crouched down and examined the sharp edge where the land dropped away. The incline had shallow steps cut out of it, too uniform to be natural, and leading down to an obvious opening in the far wall. It was perfectly round, a black disc in the otherwise sandy-brown rock.

"A hole in the Earth," Trafalgar said with wariness. "Nothing good ever comes from entering a hole in the Earth."

Dorothy stood and brushed the dirt from her hands. "And nothing exciting ever happened to those who ignored them."

"A boring life doesn't sound like the worst thing in the world right now. But we've never backed down from a challenge before." She turned to Rami. "If we're not back in an hour, contact—"

"Oh, no, I'm coming with you."

"Absolutely not," Dorothy and Trafalgar said at the same time.

Rami's smile didn't waver. "Absolutely so! I've come this far, so why not? I can carry your supplies!" He picked up their bag, which was full of various tools they'd planned to take into the cavern. Hammers, spikes, chisels, anything that might come in handy during their exploration. "Besides, you're going to need help keeping this thing in line." He gestured at the golem, which had gotten out of the truck without being instructed. It stood a few feet away, looking toward them but slightly to the left as if something over the ridge had caught its attention.

Dorothy rolled her eyes. It would be nice to have someone else lugging around the tools, and she hadn't been looking forward to figuring out how to guide the golem through tight, dark caverns. She looked at Trafalgar, who shrugged her assent.

"Very well. But you touch nothing, and you follow our instructions to the letter. If we tell you to run, you get out as quickly as possible without questioning why. Is that understood, Mr. Demirel?"

He threw her a salute which was sloppy but sincere. "You have my word!"

"Fine. Bring it down with us."

Dorothy led the way, followed by Rami and the golem. Trafalgar brought up the rear, placing her feet sideways on each step and descending as slowly as possible. The golem didn't seem to have any trouble at all, marching down as easily as if it was a staircase in someone's home.

When Dorothy reached the bottom, she took the torch from her pack and leaned into the opening, shining the light down into the tunnel.

"How does it look?" Trafalgar asked.

"Narrow, but passable." She aimed the light at the walls and then up. "Oh dear."

Trafalgar's head snapped up. "I don't like the sound of that."

"No, it's nothing," Dorothy insisted. "It's just that, ah... it, ah, seems that the tunnel is too small to stand upright. We'll have to sit or lie down and slide to the bottom." She turned and raised a finger in anticipation of Trafalgar's complaint. "We can attach a rope at the surface so we can climb out if we don't find an alternative exit once we're down there."

"And if we're unable to successfully climb out?"

"Strode did. His entire team managed to get out. However they did it, he didn't find it notable enough to chronicle it in his journal entry. We knew this was a possibility. That's why we brought the ropes in the first place. It will be a little work, we'll have to exert ourselves, but I think we're up to the challenge." She looked at Rami. "If you want to stay out here to keep an eye on the rope, we would~"

"No, I can climb," he said.

Dorothy resisted the urge to shake her head. Apparently there was just no getting away from the man. "Fantastic," she said. "Help us set up the stakes. We have to be certain the rope is absolutely secure before any of us go down."

Getting the rope in place was the work of a few minutes, but both women were sweating by the time it was ready. Dorothy wiped the sweat from her brow as she tugged on the rope and looked back at the entrance. "Shall I go first, since this whole thing is my idea?"

"I was about to suggest that very thing," Trafalgar said.

Dorothy climbed up on the lip of the entrance, positioned herself so that her feet were in the opening, and tilted forward. The slope was gradual enough that she could scoot down rather than giving in to a freefall. She leaned back at an awkward angle, her spine protesting at the strange position following the hard work of hammering in the spike on the surface. Sweat tickled her brow and dampened the collar of her shirt as she eased her way down.

When she reached the far opening, she estimated the ramp was approximately forty-five feet from end to end. She dropped her feet down, holding herself in place until she felt solid ground, then lowered herself the rest of the way into a pitch black chamber. She unhooked her flashlight again and shone it around to get a feel for where she was.

"We have a chamber," she called back up to the surface. "One opening in the northern wall, rectangular in shape. Obviously hand-carved, which is a good sign. Send the golem down, and then follow."

She heard movement from above. Less than a minute later, Trafalgar said, "Damn it! Dorothy, watch out!"

Dorothy stepped out of the way just as the golem shot out of the ramp as if he had been thrown down. She assumed the dumb thing had dived headfirst into the opening. It made a certain kind of stupid sense. It didn't have skin to protect, it didn't have to worry about tearing its clothing, and it couldn't be killed by the blunt force of slamming its head into the wall. But damn it, if everything went according to plan, this body was supposed to belong to Beatrice. She wished whatever magic had animated the thing would treat it with more respect.

"Is it all right?" Trafalgar called.

Dorothy crouched next to the golem and quickly examined it. "Hard to say," she admitted, "but it's in one piece and seems to be waiting for the next instruction."

"Rami is coming down next."

"Tell him to be a little more careful, would you?"

Rami called, "I will be very cautious!"

It took him longer than it had taken Dorothy. She used the time to explore where the opening in the wall led. She didn't venture far, never letting the opening out of her sight. By the time she returned to the main room, Trafalgar had arrived.

"I can hear water." She struggled to keep her voice steady. "This way."

Trafalgar brushed the dirt from the back of her pants and gestured for the golem to go first. Apparently that was all the instruction it required.

Dorothy didn't wait for them. She led the way into what she was calling a corridor. It was wider than the main room, but the ceiling was lower. She followed the sound of the water, wishing she had the patience to examine the carvings on the wall. This had obviously been a temple of some kind. The difficulty in reaching the Resurrection Baths had to be part of the ritual. Only people who were worthy, who were willing to go to these lengths, deserved the gift of bringing their loved one back to life.

The corridor ahead widened so that the beam of her torch didn't quite reach the opposite walls. There was also a series of archways carved into the rock. Beyond, the sound of running water was almost deafening. Her hand made the beam of the torch shake as she approached. The walls of the main cavern shined bright blue, as if the stone had its own power source that came on when it sensed their arrival.

"You didn't think we would let you get away with this, did you?"

Dorothy's smile collapsed and she turned to look at Trafalgar. "Pardon...?"

Trafalgar's chin was down, glaring hard at Dorothy. Her lips were pulled back in a snarl that made her look ugly as sin.

"Foolish, selfish Boone," Trafalgar said in a voice so unlike her own that, for a moment, Dorothy thought someone else must have been standing behind her.

Rami was standing beside Trafalgar and looked at her with a matching expression of anger and disgust. Dorothy turned to face them fully.

"What on earth are you talking about? What's gotten into you?"

Trafalgar stepped forward. "We never thought you would make it this far."

Rami said, "I told you we should have just killed her in London."

Trafalgar turned and growled at him. Rami hissed and crossed his arms over his chest, his shoulders hunched up by his ears.

Dorothy was absolutely flummoxed. "What is happening," she

whispered, asking herself as if she could prompt her mind to come up with the answer. She backed away. Trafalgar and Rami advanced, keeping the distance between them the same. The golem loomed behind them. It had no features but she had a feeling that, if it did, its eyes would match the hatred she saw in the others.

"You've come far enough, Lady Boone," Rami said.

He had acquired a new accent. And now that she'd noticed it, she realized Trafalgar's voice had changed as well. Where had she heard that... the Belgian Congo. She had spent a month there trying to gain the trust of the villagers who had known the previous water elemental, one of the women who had joined with Beatrice to become void.

"You're Kumona Majambu." Dorothy nodded at Rami. "And that accent doesn't sound particularly Russian, so that would make you Nasim Turan, the wind elemental. Is that right?" She didn't wait for a response, nodding at the golem. "Looks like you're stuck with the worst host, Oksana. Shame. I seem to remember you were the nicest one. A fan of mine, actually."

Trafalgar said, "It's no surprise you're clever. We've been observing you, Lady Boone."

"Ready to step in if it looked like you were close to a solution."

Dorothy's optimism spiked. "So I'm close."

"As close as you're going to get," Kumona-as-Trafalgar said. "When it didn't work, she screamed so loud. It was a wail unlike anything I've ever heard."

"Trafalgar tried to soothe her, but she was lost to her grief. Her pain."

"I should have stopped her."

"There was no time." Nasim shook Rami's head. "She just ran over the edge. Happened so fast. She didn't even scream."

Kumona tapped Trafalgar's temple. "Before we go, we'll make sure they actually believe they saw it. To them, it will be the truth."

Dorothy swallowed hard, trying to find the way out of this situation. Her options were horribly limited. She didn't have any weapons and, even if she did, she couldn't imagine herself injuring Trafalgar or Rami enough to stop any attacks they might level at her. She looked over her shoulder into the cavern.

"Trix has been leaving me clues. Proof she's still out there somewhere. That she exists. I assume she was doing that without you knowing."

Trafalgar looked like she'd bitten into something sour. "We knew."

"We've been one since the last time we existed on the physical plane," Rami said. "She could not act without us knowing about it. We allowed it because it was easier than stopping her."

"We allowed it because we knew that if we tried to stop her, she would only try something else. It kept her appeased and silent."

Dorothy stepped closer to them. "Does that mean she's here? Right now?"

Kumona and Nasim looked at each other, a silent exchange taking place between them before they looked back at her.

"She is here."

"And you believe she's just going to let you kill me?" Dorothy laughed and held her hands out. "Well, if that's true, then... then I suppose she's changed. She's not the person I thought she was. And beyond that, she's not a person worth bringing back. So I guess that~" She choked and put a hand to her throat. She stumbled, winced, and then said, "All right, you made your damn point."

Kumona tensed. "Oh hell."

Dorothy put her hand against the wall to support herself, breathing heavily. She felt as if she had just run ten miles in August. The cavern had been much cooler than the surface, but now the sweat burst free of her forehead and ran down the side of her face, over her jaw.

"How are you doing this? Same way they are. I'm burning up." She tugged at the top buttons of her blouse. "Yes, this is a very stressful situation for your body to be in. Trafalgar and Rami are feeling the same heat, but the spirits are suppressing it. They cannot be held long before there's permanent damage."

Dorothy squeezed her eyes shut. Both voices were hers, but she was only contributing half the conversation. Her lips and tongue moved on their own, and she heard the answers to her own questions. She focused hard, swaying to the side. She put her hand against the stone wall and rested her forehead against her fingers. She needed to ground herself and shut out everything else to focus on the voice she was hearing.

"Trix."

"I'm here."

Dorothy trembled with a wave of cold followed by a burst of heat. "God, this is unbearable. If you want me to stop, tell me. Just... just tell me to stop and I'll... go home..."

"I can't ask you to give up your life for mine."

Before Dorothy could respond to that, her shoulder was grabbed by a powerful hand. She was pulled away from the wall and tossed onto the ground.

"As touching as this is," Kumona said as she stepped over Dorothy's fallen body, "it would be kinder to do this quickly."

Dorothy rolled to the side, knocking Kumona's leg out of her way. Kumona tumbled, and Dorothy hoped Trafalgar wouldn't be too upset about any scrapes or bruises she might acquire in the fall. Before she could get to her feet, Nasim had pounced onto her back. She wrapped one arm around Dorothy's neck and pulled the wrist with her other hand, cutting off her hair. Dorothy grabbed Nasim's forearm, sent a mental apology to Rami, and threw her whole weight backward into the stone wall. Nasim exhaled explosively outward and her arm went limp, freeing Dorothy to dive forward.

The golem lunged at her. Dorothy sidestepped its lumbering steps and found herself wrapped in a bear hug by Kumona.

"You cannot win this fight," Kumona hissed in Trafalgar's voice. "How do you fight people you don't want to damage?"

"There's damage," Dorothy granted, "and then there's *damage*..."

Dorothy still had enough range of movement to reach up and dig her fingernails into the back of Kumona's hands. Kumona cried out and tried to hold on, but Dorothy dug harder and finally forced her to let go. Dorothy dropped down, threw herself forward, and grabbed the bag of supplies Nasim had dropped. She fished out one of the hammers and got back to her feet.

"And I only care about not hurting two of you." She swung the hammer as hard as she could at the golem's face. The clay was hard enough that it cracked, but it didn't shatter as she'd hoped. So she dropped the hammer, grabbed the head with both hands, and pulled with all her strength. The neck snapped, and the whole weight of the golem tumbled to the side. It slammed into Nasim, who had just gotten back to her feet, pinning her against the wall.

"Well," Dorothy said, still cradling the golem's head. "That evens the odds a little bit."

Kumona examined the bloody back of her hand. "That golem was your ticket to reviving Bao Tai Sek. You've already lost."

"I'm Lady Dorothy Boone. And that body you're misusing is Trafalgar Rhys. We don't accept defeat, not when we're both still standing."

Kumona arched an eyebrow. "Then this should be an interesting fight."

Dorothy winked and threw the golem's head. Kumona sidestepped it, but the head was only a distraction so Dorothy could stoop down and grab the supply bag again. Kumona rushed forward. Dorothy got out what she wanted and threw the bag underhand so it would hit Kumona center-mass. She hit her target and Kumona doubled over, one of the hammers dropping onto her foot.

"Sorry, Trav," Dorothy said, adopting Violet's pet name as she threaded the rope she'd recovered through her hands. If she could just get close enough to wrap the rope around Kumona's arms, she could restrain her long enough to achieve her goal. "Hopefully you'll forgive a few superficial wounds."

Kumona said, "Perhaps I'll just bash her head against the stone until you concede. Go on. Throw yourself off that cliff over there or I'll spill her brains all over this cavern."

"No, Kumona, you won't," Dorothy said, but she only heard the words as they came out of her mouth. "You're not a murderer. You're not cruel. And you won't kill someone in cold blood."

Kumona narrowed her eyes. "We knew what would be asked of us when we created Void. Maybe not exactly, but we knew. Just as surely as the rest of us knew we had to be in London on a certain date, in a specific place. It's why we were born. We fulfilled our promise."

"And now we simply fade away?" Beatrice asked. "I do not accept that. I did my part, but I have a life. And I want my life back."

"If our selfishness undoes the Void, what then?"

"You are not your abilities," Dorothy said. She felt an odd lump in her throat and wondered if that was something Beatrice was trying to say. "You were elementals. You used your powers for their intended purpose, but that isn't all you were. I learned about all of you. Your people loved you, Kumona. And..." She turned to look at the inert golem. "Oksana loved the people of her village enough to keep them warm through the harsh winters."

Nasim, still pinned, snorted. "My people didn't love me. They would have killed me if they didn't think I was the Devil."

"But you still protected them," Dorothy said. "You watched over them, didn't you? They called you a demon and djinn, but you guarded them from danger just the same."

Nasim looked away.

"You were all hosts for the elemental power. You delivered that power where it was needed. If there's a chance, any chance at all, that you can be brought back... don't you deserve that? You saved the world. Surely you should be allowed to live in it."

There was conflict in Kumona's features. Beatrice said, "We can come back without our power. Leave it behind. Just be... ordinary."

"Never ordinary," Dorothy said softly, and her lips curled into a smile.

The tension in Kumona's shoulders relaxed. Not much, but enough to give Dorothy hope.

"Do you honestly believe you can do this?"

"I believe she can," Beatrice said.

Kumona grimaced and looked away. She suddenly slumped to one side, just barely getting her hand up in time to prevent herself from smacking her head against the stone.

"Good lord," Trafalgar whispered. Even from those two words, Dorothy could somehow tell that the former elemental had released her. She looked up with wide, unfocused eyes as if she had just woken up. "Dorothy..."

"You were taken over~"

"I remember. I was aware." She put a hand to her temple. "I was conscious, I just couldn't... control anything." She turned her hand around and examined the wounds. "I won't hold this against you. Just as you wouldn't blame me if our positions had been reversed."

"Glad to hear it."

Rami cleared his throat. "And, ah...! I will not be angry about being pinned beneath this thing if one of you..."

"Crumbs," Dorothy muttered, rushing to his aid. It took both her and Trafalgar working together to lift the now-lifeless creature enough for him to scurry out. "Are you all right?"

"Nothing permanently hurt." He brushed himself off and looked around as if he expected to see ghosts swirling around. "Are they... um... still...?"

"Yes," Beatrice said. "They've been following me since we left London. And I've never left your side, Dorothy."

Dorothy looked at the ground, as if there was some way to avoid the gaze of someone who was sharing her eyes. "I did things I'm ashamed of..."

"You weren't yourself," Beatrice said.

Trafalgar looked at the golem. "You destroyed it. That was..."

"Just a contingency," Dorothy said. "We were never certain we actually needed it."

"But there has to be a body."

Dorothy walked past her without answering. The ground sloped away from where the fight had occurred, leading down into what was obviously the main chamber. Dorothy went down without looking back, and Trafalgar sighed, following her.

"What do I do?" Rami asked.

"Stay there," Trafalgar and Dorothy said at the same time.

The chamber was a huge well, with a series of stone steps carved into the wall a central pool. Dorothy estimated it was approximately fifty feet deep and an equal distance across. She followed the angled ground toward the waterfall which fed the water below. The water coursed down, passing through the glowing stones in several places before it finally plummeted down to the pool. Dorothy's path ended at a wider area which almost looked like a naturally occurring shower stall. It was partially enclosed, with small openings at the top and bottom where the water could pass over anyone standing in its way.

"This is it," Dorothy said. "All I have to do is stand here and let the water pass over me..."

"And you're certain that's what you wish to do?"

Dorothy looked at her, already unbuttoning her blouse. "Of course. Without question or hesitation. Did you think I'd come this far just to have second thoughts? Beatrice is *here*. You just heard her!"

"I heard a convincing puppet show," Trafalgar said.

"Are you denying you were possessed by Kumona?"

"No. No, that was definitely, and disturbingly, real." She looked at the water. Something about it did seem strange. But perhaps that was just her expectations coloring her observations. She knew the water was supposed to have magical properties so it looked exotic. "I only question whether... whether you've truly thought through the risks."

"There's no risk for me." Dorothy shrugged out of her blouse and carefully folded it. She handed it to Trafalgar and undid her belt. "Immortal. Remember?"

"And I'm sure you recall there's no effective test to prove immortality. We only have the word of Riya Lennox, a woman we know has stretched the truth to serve her ultimate goals. Are you willing to put your life at risk based on her word?"

Dorothy stepped out of her trousers. Trafalgar took them as well. Dorothy stood next to the waterfall in her brassiere and tap pants, pondering the question. Finally she looked at Trafalgar with tears in her eyes.

"Beatrice never asked me to explain myself. She never asked me to prove my beliefs beyond a shadow of a doubt, or explain a threat so she could decide if it was worth joining the fight. My fights were hers, and she fought just as I said. Without question or hesitation. She protected us. Defended us. She put everything, every piece of herself, into our fight. She believed in us. So no matter what happens when I step into that water, I'm only doing what Beatrice would have done for either of us."

Trafalgar nodded and took a step back. "Then I won't stop you, Dorothy."

Dorothy nodded and held out her hand. "If this is the last time we speak, I want you to know I'm sorry. I regret the partnership we lost, and the years we could have had together."

Trafalgar took Dorothy's hand and squeezed it. "I didn't have to let you go. I'm as much to blame for the end of our partnership as you are."

"I'll forgive you, if you forgive me."

"Seems like a good deal." Trafalgar let her hand linger in Dorothy's for another moment, then let her go. "Bring our Beatrice back to us, Lady Boone."

Dorothy nodded and faced forward. She took a deep breath, held her head up high, and stepped into the waterfall.

CHAPTER FOURTEEN

THE WATER almost froze her face as it washed over her features, chilling her entire body in one sweep. Gooseflesh rose on her arms and chest, and she instinctively crossed her arms over her chest. She remained as upright as possible and tilted her head up so the water would pass over her face. It didn't take her long to get acclimated to the temperature, though she knew her hands were still trembling. Her hands felt like ice and she tucked them under her arms. She kept her eyes closed and waited.

"Dorothy?" Trafalgar sounded miles away on the other side of the water. "Can you feel anything happening?"

"I don't know. I don't know if it's supposed to feel like anyth~" Her voice was choked off by the sudden and complete change in the water's temperature. Suddenly, cold became scalding, and her body tensed in preparation to flee. She curled her toes on the stone and managed to stay where she was, but she hunched forward and managed to squeak out a cry.

"Dorothy?"

She couldn't answer because anything she tried to say would only come out as a screech. It felt as if the water was flaying her. It was sheer agony, in every muscle and bone.

She felt inhuman, just a pile of parts held together by electricity, and the water was breaking those bonds one at a time. She had never feared being shattered like a piece of glass but now she could tell that was how her life was going to end.

It was clear to Trafalgar that Dorothy was in the midst of some kind of tremendous pain. Her face was twisted in a mask of sheer agony, and her face was disturbingly red. She stepped forward with the intention of pulling her free, but movement in the corner of her eye stopped her. She looked down into the pool below and saw a shape rising in the water. No... the water was flowing *around* something, a transparent object that disrupted the flow and then... no, it wasn't transparent anymore. She could see skin tone, the line of a muscle.

Trafalgar's eyes widened. She'd seen so many miraculous things, but this was a new height.

"My god. It's working..."

"Dorothy!" Trafalgar's shout echoed through the water. "It's working!"

Dorothy opened her eyes. That was all she needed to hear to withstand the pain, even though now it felt like the fire was coming from inside her body. Her hands were curled into claws and a panicked, animal part of her mind wanted to tear her skin off so it would stop hurting so damned much. But through her tears and the flowing water, she could see Trafalgar had moved to the edge of the platform and was looking down. A moment later, Trafalgar grabbed one of their bags and took off at a run.

It was working. She just had to endure it a little longer...

Trafalgar raced down the inclined path, down to the pool, watching her step but also keeping an eye on the body now floating face-down in the water. She reached the edge of the pool and stopped, unsure of what she should do. If she moved before the process was done, would she simply pull a corpse back to shore? If she delayed, would Beatrice be resurrected only to drown? She was naked at the moment, and the most striking thing Trafalgar noticed was the fact she was missing the massive tree tattoo that had once stretched the length of her spine.

There was a full body now. Her hair spread around her head and she was completely still.

Trafalgar looked back up to the waterfall. Dorothy was still standing, though the shape of her was completely enshrouded by water now. If she didn't pull Beatrice from the water, would the pain continue until Dorothy succumbed? How was she supposed to know how long to wait? And if she was wrong, did she risk losing them both?

"How long, Dorothy?" Trafalgar whispered. "How long am I supposed to wait before I act?"

The change was as drastic as it had been the first time, but it took Dorothy a few seconds to realize she was no longer in pain. The water felt like a soothing balm on her suffering flesh, like a bucket of rainwater dumped on a wildfire. She stumbled forward and her foot, slick from being submerged, skidded out from underneath her. She tumbled hard and just barely managed to break her fall with both hands, lowering her head gently to the gloriously cold stone. She couldn't catch her breath, and her eyelids felt too heavy to open.

But that was fine. The pain was over. She could just lie here for a few minutes.

Trafalgar didn't hesitate when she saw Dorothy fall. She dropped the bag and ran into the water, praying it was as shallow as it seemed to be. It was up to her waist when she reached Beatrice. She wrapped her arms around the floating woman's torso and lifted her face up out of the water before she moved backward toward the shore. Beatrice was heavier than Trafalgar expected, and completely dead weight dragging in the water.

"Come on, Beatrice, don't let us down now. We've come this far, my love."

When she reached the edge of the water, she laid Beatrice out on the stone and knelt next to her. She placed her hands on Beatrice's chest but before she could begin compressions, Beatrice jerked and arched her back, rolling to one side and spitting up a mouthful of water. Trafalgar put her hand on Beatrice's shoulder.

"Are you all right, darling? It's all right. Take your time. Breathe."

"Trafalgar...?"

"That's right." She rubbed Beatrice's arm. "What do you remember?"

Beatrice coughed and pushed herself up. "Everything. Where's

Dorothy?"

Trafalgar looked up toward the waterfall, dreading the answer to that question.

"Bloody waste of time, waiting for a cab every time I want to go somewhere." Dorothy was outside herself, watching from over her own shoulder as she pulled on a pair of gloves. *"Easier just to walk."*

"Easier to buy a car. You can afford it."

"Obviously. But I have neither the time nor patience to learn how to drive."

Beatrice stepped into her line of sight. Still a new addition to the household, still seeing Dorothy as an employer rather than anything else. *"Even I know how to drive."*

"Well, bully for you."

Beatrice smiled. *"I meant I could drive you where you needed to go. As needed."*

Dorothy paused in her preparations. *"Really?"*

"I like driving. We could add it to my household duties."

"If it wouldn't be an imposition..."

Beatrice smiled. *"I owe you my life, Lady Boone."*

"Dorothy. Lady Boone makes me sound like I'm your superior."

"Aren't you?"

Dorothy laughed. *"That's not the kind of relationship I want to have with anyone, Ms. Sek."*

"You can call me Beatrice. Or Trix, if you like."

"Trix!" Dorothy laughed again. *"Oh, that is delightful! Trix. I love it. All right, Trix, look into getting us a car. Get one you like. I'm just going to be the passenger."*

"As you wish... Dorothy."

The hallway morphed into Dorothy's bedroom. Beatrice was lying next to Dorothy, both of them still dressed.

"We can just lie here like this until we fall asleep, if that's what you're comfortable with," Dorothy said. Her voice sounded incredibly loud in the dark room.

"I don't think that would be very satisfying for either of us."

"Speak for yourself, Trix," Dorothy said, touching Beatrice's cheek. *"I could stare at this face for the rest of my days and never get bored."*

"I've never done anything like this in my life," Beatrice said, and Dorothy remembered it was the third or fourth time she'd mentioned it.

"I know, darling. We can go as slowly as you need."

"No, you're..." She took Dorothy's hand, kissed the palm. *"I've spent my whole life not doing what we're about to do. And I think I've wasted enough time."*

"Ah... I see." Dorothy closed the distance and kissed her.

More scenes from their life together flooded Dorothy's mind. Cozy dinners, long and quiet drives to one town or another. She saw them eating dinner together in a little French hostel after a mission, the room lit by candles and smelling of smoke from the fireplace. She saw Beatrice tending her bruised knuckles, a scraped palm, a minor knife wound. She felt soft kisses placed on her cheek, forehead, the corner of her mouth, her closed eyelids.

"Dorothy?"

"Bea..." Her voice failed her and her eyes struggled to open. When she finally managed the massive feat, they couldn't focus on anything. She saw blobs of light and color until soft fingers swept across her face and cleared away the massive amount of water that had apparently accumulated over her eyes. She felt half-drowned but she was on solid ground and she could breathe, and someone had lifted her up onto their lap so she wasn't on her back.

"Did it work?" Her voice was rough from the choked screaming. "Trafalgar?"

"It worked." Beatrice's voice made Dorothy's heart skip, and then it soared when Beatrice's lips covered her own. Dorothy whimpered and found the strength to reach up and put her hand on the back of Beatrice's head. "I love you," Beatrice said.

"I love you," Dorothy echoed, now able to see for herself that she was indeed lying in the lap of the woman she loved. She was wearing a dress shirt, but she hadn't taken the time to button it. Her skin was more ashen than she remembered, but she assumed that was a byproduct of the seven years that had passed since she'd seen the sun. "You're alive."

Beatrice smiled. "Thanks to you."

Dorothy touched Beatrice's cheek. "I don't know what I'm going to dream about now."

Beatrice laughed, and tears rolled down her cheeks. "I'm sure we can think of something together. Can you stand?"

Trafalgar came closer. "I can help you both. We can get Rami down to help you out~"

"No." Dorothy struggled to get up. "There's something I must do first."

"You've done enough," Trafalgar said.

Dorothy couldn't catch her breath, but she was back on her feet. She shook her head and pointed at the waterfall with a trembling hand.

"Take me back."

"Absolutely not! What in the world for?"

"Kumona," Dorothy said. "Nasim. Oksana."

Trafalgar was sure she'd misheard. "The women who, moments ago, tried to *kill* both of us? Are you insane? And look at the state of you. You're lucky you survived bringing Beatrice back."

"I proved it was possible. I proved I could survive. No one is supposed to survive. Ergo, Riya was telling the truth and I'm immortal. It won't be pleasant, but it won't kill me."

"Or it will simply make you wish you were dead," Trafalgar said.

Dorothy swallowed the lump in her throat and shook her head. "We owe this to them. They gave everything to save the world. If I can bring them back, even if it costs me everything..."

Beatrice said, "Dorothy, I just got you back..."

"I know, my love. I know." She looked at Beatrice and her heart broke at the idea of leaving her. "But it's the right thing to do. And you've spent the past seven years tangled up with them. Do you believe they would just leave us alone after this? They've shown their power. They can possess any one of us, or Violet, or a member of the Society, and cause untold amounts of havoc if we leave them behind."

Beatrice rested her forehead against Dorothy's, then looked at Trafalgar. "She's right. They'd never leave us alone. This way, they will be in our debt. They can go home, go back to their lives."

Trafalgar looked at the waterfall. "Maybe one of us—"

"It would kill anyone else. It nearly killed me."

"Even immortality must have limits."

Dorothy exhaled sharply. It was hard for her to stand, but she leaned on Trafalgar. "I know. I know. Trix, when you and the other elementals created the Void, you knew there was likely no coming back from it. You all did it anyway. Without hesitation."

Beatrice closed her eyes. "I love you, Dorothy."

"I love you, Bao Tai Sek."

"She has no choice, Trafalgar." Beatrice was crying openly now. "It's the right thing to do."

Trafalgar clenched her jaw. "Then I have no choice but to be at her side while she does it."

Dorothy looked at Trafalgar, too grateful to put it into words.

"I should have been at your side this whole time, Dorothy. I allowed my anger to keep me away. Maybe if I'd forced myself back into your life sooner, we could have gotten to this point years ago. As it is, standing watch while you risk your life is the least I can do."

"Thank you, my friend. I love you, too."

"And I love you, Dorothy. Now come on."

Together, Trafalgar and Beatrice took Dorothy back to the waterfall. "Don't let the water touch your skin, either of you," she warned. "We don't know what it will do to anyone else."

Trafalgar squeezed Dorothy's hand. "Whatever happens next... Violet and I will take care of you. If you survive and are... diminished in some way, or if you die and arrangements have to be made, we will make sure you are taken care of."

Dorothy smiled. "Of course you will. That's what family does."

She leaned in and kissed Trafalgar's lips, looked one last time at Beatrice, and then backed up into flow of the waterfall.

Her screams began a moment later.

Chapter Fifteen

Dorothy opened her eyes. She was being held in someone's lap, her head on their shoulder. Beatrice. She knew the smell of her lover, and she snuggled her face into the material of her dress shirt. They were both swaying side to side in a gentle rhythm. It was almost enough to put her to sleep but she forced herself to take stock of her surroundings first. She was facing the driver, Rami, who looked like he was in a splendid kind of shock. His eyes were wide, his mouth open and smiling, as if all his brain power was occupied by processing what he'd seen in the caves.

Dorothy shifted her head to look over Beatrice's shoulder, out the back window. Trafalgar and Oksana were sitting against one sidewall of the truck bed, their feet alternating with Kumona and Nasim who were sat on the other side. They all looked utterly exhausted, shell-shocked. The three former elementals were dressed very skimpily in clothes that had been borrowed from Trafalgar and apparently Rami, who she now noticed was in his undershirt.

"I survived," Dorothy said, her voice raspy.

"We know, love," Beatrice whispered, stroking Dorothy's hair. She had been holding her head to one side, where the sun would fall on her face. Now she looked down and met Dorothy's gaze, smiling with relief. "But it's nice of you to wake up to confirm it." She kissed Dorothy's forehead. "Go back to sleep."

She didn't want to sleep. She wanted to stare at Beatrice, wanted to lock her face in her mind. But she really was extraordinarily tired, and she was being held in strong arms, and Beatrice's scent was intoxicating. The truck swayed and Dorothy's eyes drifted shut again.

In the end it was just easier to give in and sleep for a little while longer.

She slept for an entire day before regaining enough strength to drink some water and eat a meal. Araminta made the decision to remain docked in case Dorothy - or one of their unexpected new passengers - required medical assistance. Dorothy woke up a few times to find Beatrice in the room with her. Once curled up beside her, and twice carefully placing a tray of food on the side table. When she finally woke up and felt confident she could stay conscious, Beatrice was staring out the porthole. She was wearing a shirt and trousers that Dorothy remembered packing in her own suitcase.

Dorothy pushed herself up to rest against the headboard. "What's so fascinating out there?"

"The world," Beatrice said with a smile. "It looks so different... where I've been. Or looking at it the way I'd grown accustomed to. We couldn't feel the sun on our face. The wind. The smells. It's like someone turned every sense back on." She came to the bed and sat down, reaching out to stroke Dorothy's hair, surreptitiously feeling her forehead for a temperature. "How do you feel?"

"Much better than I did a few hours ago." She looked at Beatrice's clothes. "Or... yesterday?"

"It was yesterday," Beatrice confirmed. "I'm not going to lie. There were moments when none of us had much faith you'd wake up. Your skin was cold to the touch, and it had turned grey. But there was a pulse, albeit faint, and your breath fogged a mirror."

"You did the mirror test? Blimey." She found Beatrice's hand, holding it tightly. "I'm glad you held onto hope. How do I look now?"

Beatrice's eyes softened, and her voice was so quiet Dorothy almost didn't hear it. "Beautiful. Your color has been improving. Do you think you can eat a little?"

"No, I think I could eat a feast. I'm absolutely starved."

"Fantastic news." Beatrice got up and retrieved the food she'd brought in. It was a bowl of soup, crackers, and an egg salad sandwich. Dorothy picked up one half of the sandwich and destroyed it in three bites. Beatrice went to fill a glass of water, and the other half of the sandwich was gone by the time she got back. "Easy, now," Beatrice said. "Don't get everyone's hopes up just to choke now."

Dorothy nodded and moved the soup bowl closer. "What have I missed?"

"Trafalgar convinced Minty to extend our trip. We're taking the other elementals back home."

"Good lord. That has to be over ten thousand miles."

Beatrice nodded. "Her navigator is plotting the course now. It's going to extend our return to London by... quite a... considerable length, but Minty thinks it's a small price to pay for what the four of us did for the world. She doesn't want them to wait a moment longer than necessary to be home again."

"I definitely owe her. And her crew." She carefully sipped her soup and closed her eyes. "Mm. Splendid. Absolutely wonderful, Trix."

"It's been a while since I cooked for you, but I remember the basics."

Dorothy stirred her spoon through the soup. "I could feel you with me. Watching over me. Telling me I was on the right path."

Something changed in Beatrice's eyes. She looked away, but not before Dorothy could see it.

"What?"

"Nothing..." She sighed and rolled her head on her shoulders. "I'm sorry, Dorothy. But you misunderstood what I was trying to say with the dirt."

Dorothy blanched. "Oh no."

"I was trying to say let me go. To bury me before the obsession buried you. Even after I realized you were taking it the wrong way, even after I saw how far you were willing to take things, I couldn't find a way to make myself clear. I thought about possessing you, but it seemed like too much of a violation. Of course that all changed when Kumona crossed the line first. But Dorothy..." She reached out and took her hand. "I don't want you to think I'm ungrateful. You brought me back. You saved me. I'll be forever in your debt for that."

"We don't have debts," Dorothy said. "Not with each other."

Beatrice brought Dorothy's hand up to kiss the fingers. "I should go tell the others you're awake and eating. They'll be relieved."

"Wait," Dorothy said. "I'm still feeling a bit groggy. Let me rest for another half hour before you bring them all in here so they can start fussing over me."

"I suppose that's a reasonable request."

"And will you lie down with me?"

Beatrice smiled. She removed the food tray, carrying it to the side table before she came back and stretched out next to Dorothy. They wrapped their arms around each other and scooted closer until there was no more room between them.

When Araminta was convinced that Dorothy was recovered enough to fly, she had her crew set a course to start taking their passengers home. The trip was easy to plot out since it was very similar to the journey they'd taken Dorothy on years ago when she had first researched the elementals. The only difference was their point of origin but that was an easy enough adjustment.

The *Skylarker* headed to Africa first, a straight southerly shot across the Sahara to the Belgian Congo. Halfway through the journey, Dorothy was pacing the length of her room to build her strength back up when there was a knock on the door. She'd been expecting Trafalgar to she answered without checking to see who the guest was. Of all the people aboard the ship, Kumona was the last person she would have expected to see.

"Oh. Hello."

"Lady Boone," Kumona said softly. "I have spent the time since our resurrection trying to think of a way to express my~"

Dorothy held up her hand. "Bygones."

Kumona frowned, lines appearing above her eyebrows. "I tried to kill you. I threatened the lives of your compatriots. The only reason I am standing here now is because Beatrice warned you that we would have been like poltergeists..."

"That's not why I brought you back," Dorothy interrupted. "I did it because it was the right thing to do. As for the fight, you were frightened. You thought I was trying to undo the very good thing you had done with your sacrifice, so you lashed out. If our positions had been reversed, I'm not certain I would have acted differently."

"That's very gracious of you," Kumona said. "But I hope you will still accept my apology."

"Consider it accepted."

Kumona inclined her head. "Thank you, Lady Boone."

"Dorothy."

"Dorothy."

They spent most of the day over the desert. They landed, and

Kumona bid a very fond farewell to the women she'd spent the past seven years existing with. Dorothy was still uncertain about what, exactly, that existence had been like. Beatrice tried to explain it but she lacked the words.

"We were conscious, and aware of the world around us. And we were still ourselves. But we were also united. We were a single being. But not in the way you would imagine a... a person or an entity." She'd finally given up and shook her head in frustration. "It's not anything you can explain or understand without experiencing it. And I have no intention of ever going back to that state, so I don't think it's necessary to revisit the sensations of it."

Dorothy agreed and let the subject drop. Still, she had to confess a certain amount of curiosity on the subject.

Once they'd delivered Kumona to her home, the *Skylarker* headed north to Persia. The situation in the country wasn't as volatile as it had once been, but Araminta still warned her crew and passengers to be prepared for some dicey flying to avoid any confrontations. The two-day flight across the Arabian peninsula was tense and Dorothy doubted any of them got much sleep. Fortunately their precautions were unnecessary and they were spared from violence, landing at a location near the Caspian Sea without incident. Nasim had spent the entire trip isolated from everyone else but, before she left, she approached Dorothy and held out her hand.

"Thank you." She kept her eyes on the ground. "I know you suffered for my life. Kumona said you refused any kind of reward or gratitude for the sacrifice, but I wanted you to know it was not... I will not forget it."

Dorothy shook her hand. "It was an honor. And thank you for your sacrifice."

Nasim nodded, looked around the ship one last time, and then departed.

Their next leg was the shortest, just a quick twenty-hour hop into a remote area of western Russia. They had refueled at each of their last stops but their destination in Russia didn't have any sort of amenities waiting for them. They had to stock up in Persia and hope they had enough to make the rest of the trip without going out of their way to stop somewhere in Europe to top themselves up. Araminta was confident they had enough fuel, and Dorothy trusted her enough to share in that confidence, but the captain had also added, "It could be tight. A little tight. But definitely doable."

When they landed in Russia, Oksana surprised Dorothy with a hug. "I am still a very avid appreciator of what you do, Lady Boone. I am sorry for finding ourselves on opposite sites recently. Is why I chose the creature without eyes or face when we fought. I was glad when you crushed its head."

"I hope it didn't hurt you."

Oksana laughed. "No. Felt strange. But no hurting." She kissed Dorothy on both cheeks. "I am now a part of your story! An honor. Even if it is as a villain."

"Not a villain to me, Oksana. Never."

The Russian woman grinned, hugged Beatrice tightly, and headed out into the life she'd left behind all those years ago.

Araminta joined Dorothy at the ramp, hugging herself against the cold as they watched Oksana trudge off into the distance.

"Last leg. Time to head home."

"Mm."

"Are you ready?"

Dorothy raised an eyebrow. "Lots of apologies to be made back there."

Araminta started to say something, then stopped herself.

"What?"

Araminta shrugged. "There are apologies to be made right here on the ship. We've been flying around for most of a week. I'm sure you've noticed there's someone who has made herself scarce." She looked pointedly at Dorothy. "It's not that big of a ship."

"Ah. Yes, I was thinking I would address that when we were home."

"If you're comfortable letting it fester that long. My suggestion? Don't wait until you're back in your own home, or in hers. The *Skylarker* can be neutral territory."

Dorothy blew out air and nodded. "You have a point. Thank you."

Araminta put a hand on Dorothy's shoulder and walked away, leaving her alone. Dorothy had known this conversation had to take place. Doing it on the ship meant she wouldn't have anywhere to run. Maybe that was for the best. She'd never been a coward and she would be damned if she started acting like one now.

She straightened the cuffs of her blouse and left to go find her former partner.

CHAPTER SIXTEEN

TRAFALGAR HELD the camera up to the porthole, her finger hovering over the trigger until she was confident she could get a decent photo. She didn't know what the tall, skinny trees were actually called, but they looked like leafy spikes sticking straight up into the air. She knew Violet would be entranced by them but she wasn't confident in her photography skills. She snapped a few exposures in the hopes at least one of them would come out, then lowered the camera.

The *Skylarker* had lifted off a few minutes ago, and now began the long journey home. In something around thirty hours, she would be back in London and back in Violet's arms. She was twitchy with anticipation and hoped that hadn't affected the pictures.

She was stowing the camera in her bag when someone knocked. "Yes?"

"It's Dorothy."

Trafalgar hesitated, then stepped across the room and opened the door. Dorothy stood in front of her, hands clasped behind her back, head down.

"May I come in?"

She couldn't think of a reasonable excuse, so she nodded once and stepped to the side. "Beatrice and Araminta told me you were recovering. I was very glad to hear it. I would have come by to visit, but I've been occupying myself with making a record of the carvings and artifacts in the cave."

"I don't remember carvings or artifacts."

"Every wall was covered," Trafalgar said. "There were two small statues on either side of the waterfall. I saw you looking at them when we first..." Dorothy looked confused. "Well. You were distracted. A little brain haze is probably to be expected."

"I suppose I'll be fortunate if that's the extent of my suffering."

Trafalgar searched for something else to say. "All the elementals have been returned to their homes."

"Yes! Thank you. Beatrice told me you convinced Araminta to make the journey even though it kept you from your bride for so much longer than planned."

"Violet understood. We've spoken on the telephone at the various stops. And she always knows where I am because... well."

"Ah, yes. I'm not sure if I'd find that convenient or horrifying. I suppose you make it work."

"Mm-hmm." Trafalgar let the silence linger. Dorothy searched the room as if trying to find something else to comment on. "Why are you here, Dorothy?"

"We should probably have a conversation, don't you think?"

"About what?"

"The future. What comes next."

Trafalgar shook her head. "I'm sorry, Dorothy, but if you're talking about us, I've already made it perfectly clear that there is no 'us' moving forward. That hasn't changed."

Dorothy pressed her lips together. "I see. I thought perhaps the experience~"

"No," Trafalgar said bluntly.

"Right." Dorothy inhaled, breathed out slowly, and then nodded. "Well. If this has to be our last conversation, I want to use it to express my deep and sincere apologies for how I acted. I shut you out. I hurt you and people you care about. People we both care about. I wanted to say that I believed the ends justified the means, but that implies I actually considered my actions were wrong. At the time, I didn't. I was beyond right and wrong. I was beyond hurting people. I'm sorry, Trafalgar. I am truly and completely sorry. I hope one day you can forgive me."

She wet her lips and touched a knuckle to her eye, then stepped quickly toward the door.

"I'll leave you to your work now."

"Dorothy."

She stopped with her hand on the knob.

"Your actions nearly cost Violet her life." She snapped off the end of the last word, reined in her anger, steadied her breath. "Because of you, I looked into my wife's eyes uncertain if she would survive. I saw her blouse soaked with her blood. I can never forget that, regardless of whatever else we might have meant to each other."

"I know. And I understand, I do."

"At the same time," Trafalgar said, sinking onto the edge of her bed. "You gave me a unique perspective into your actions. I didn't know what was going to happen in the minutes after that gunshot. I didn't even remember we had a healer among our ranks. I saw blood pouring out of Violet and I wanted... I wanted to destroy the world so I wouldn't have to watch her leave it. She was still alive, she was gasping for breath but alive, and I still felt so... distraught. I was overcome with grief like I'd never known. It erased colors. Sounds. All I could feel was the pain of a world without her."

Dorothy turned to look at her.

"I can't condone what you did. And I doubt we can ever truly be partners again. But I can at least say I understand your actions. I felt your desperation. That's enough for me to put my anger aside if the need arises. We can work together, Dorothy, we can be allies. But we'll never again be partners, not the way we were."

Dorothy understood. "I'm grateful to have that much. I want... I want you to know... I love you, Trafalgar."

Trafalgar looked down at the floor. Finally, she nodded. "I love you, too. There wouldn't be this much pain if I didn't."

Dorothy smiled sadly. "Until the next time, then? Whenever that may be?"

"Until next time, Lady Boone."

"I'll be waiting, Mrs. Rhys."

Dorothy left, closing the door behind her.

Being in a body had unforeseen difficulties. It required sleep, fuel, and maintenance. For the first few days, Beatrice found herself exhausted by walking from her quarters to the kitchen to have breakfast. It didn't take her long to build her strength and stamina back up, but she also had to deal with the loss of her magic. She didn't expect it to be such a noticeable absence, let alone so similar to losing a limb. But she got used to the lack, learned to work around it, and soon she felt almost normal. It was something she hadn't considered herself in a very long time, so normal was strange.

The day they dropped off the last elemental, Oksana, she found Dorothy on the viewing deck. She joined her on the bench. She could tell Dorothy had been crying but opted not to mention it.

"How many times did you do this over the past seven years?" Dorothy asked after a long silence.

"What do you mean?"

Dorothy sniffled and wiped at her eyes. "Been near me when I was full of despair. When the pain of not having you with me was too much."

"Oh. I don't know. As often as I could."

"I thought so. I felt you there. You may have been trying to warn me away, but how could I give up when I knew you were right there next to me and I just... I couldn't quite reach you?"

Beatrice said, "I know. I understand." She reached for Dorothy's hand, stopped herself, then closed the distance and grabbed it. She inhaled sharply and squeezed. "I'm still getting used to that. Touching." She brushed her thumb across Dorothy's fingers. "Having a body again. Remembering all the sensations."

Dorothy leaned closer to her. Beatrice turned her head and held her breath. Dorothy kissed her. Neither of them had said anything about waiting, about delaying this part of their reunion, just like there was no conversation about if this was the right time. Their lips met and they knew they'd waited long enough. She heard Dorothy make a small noise, more just a tremble of her vocal chords that translated to her lips and tongue.

"I've missed you, Dorothy," Beatrice said after the kiss. "I missed being alive, but everything I missed was linked to you. Touching you, listening to you breathe, holding you."

Dorothy leaned back against the cushion. "Come here, darling."

Beatrice stood up and sat on the edge of the bench between Dorothy's legs. She leaned back and Dorothy took her weight, one hand skimming along Beatrice's thigh while the other moved up to her breast.

"Where did this body come from?" Dorothy asked.

"Manifested," Beatrice said, already breathless in anticipation. "The last bit of our magic... used to recreate our vessels as they once were."

Dorothy nipped Beatrice's ear. "And what a vessel it is." She moved her mouth down, and Beatrice gasped as her lips grazed her neck. "I would have moved heaven and Earth to have this body in my arms again..."

"You very nearly did." Dorothy's hand pressed against the crotch of her pants. Beatrice's body tensed and she cried out softly. "Dorothy..."

"This has always been my favorite position for us, Trix. Feeling your weight against me."

"I love it too."

Dorothy managed to get Beatrice's pants open. "I didn't mind having you inside of me, though. You should have tried that sooner. We could've had so much fun."

"There were nights." Beatrice opened her eyes and looked out the window. She could just barely see the treetops, and tall mountains rose in the distance, but the view was mostly of clear open skies. "I would touch your mind and send you sweet dreams. When the dreams included us, I would... I w-would bring them to the surface. And I would hold you as much as I could, watch you touch yourself without waking. It was the clo..." She grunted. Dorothy was teasing her now. "It was the closest I could get to feeling the pleasure myself."

"I remember those nights... beautiful, sweet dreams of my Trix."

"Don't stop kissing my neck, love."

Dorothy obliged. She moved her hand, then began using her fingers. Beatrice stiffened, then twisted and pressed her lips against Dorothy's hair. She'd missed the smell of Dorothy's hair. She smelled like sweat, and the strange ozone of the underground cavern. The enchanted water had been washed out during her convalescence, but Beatrice could still pick up traces of it. She had a feeling it would linger for much longer than any natural scents.

"Don't hold back, love," Dorothy whispered against the curve of her shoulder. "We'll do this properly later. But right now I just want to remind you of how good your body can feel."

"Yes," Beatrice moaned. She moved her hands to the outside of Dorothy's thighs and dug in with her fingers, lifting her hips to meet Dorothy's hand. She wanted to be naked, wanted to be skin-to-skin, to feel the heat shared between them, but she also didn't want to stop long enough to make that happen. She couldn't stop, not now. She felt herself on the edge and rocked her hips faster. Dorothy responded by pressing harder, and Beatrice cried out.

Dorothy shushed her, then nipped the shell of her ear. "I've missed you so much, Beatrice." The pad of one finger, wet and firm, pressed against her clit and made Beatrice's heels tap against the floor. "My Trix, my love..."

"Please, Dorothy." She closed her eyes and moved one hand to press it against Dorothy's. "Please, yes..." She bit her bottom lip and twisted until she could see Dorothy's face. She had looked into these eyes so many times over the past few years. They'd always looked through her, past her. But now they were looking directly at her, and Beatrice shuddered on the edge of her orgasm.

"Do you see me?"

"I see you, Beatrice." One finger slipped inside of her, then another. "I want to see you."

Beatrice cried out, and this time Dorothy didn't shush her. She stiffened and climaxed against Dorothy's hand. She shuddered, face twisted in what looked like pain until she gasped and relaxed. She slumped in Dorothy's arms, and Dorothy took her weight. Her nerves were on fire, she was panting for breath, and her skin was hot. She was alive. She was human, she had a body, and she could feel. Her heart pounded in the aftermath of her orgasm, her first orgasm in years, and proof she had truly survived her ordeal.

Dorothy kissed Beatrice's cheek, her neck, and held her tightly so she wouldn't slip down onto the floor. When Beatrice caught her breath, she turned to look at Dorothy again.

"This can't be very comfortable for you."

"I want to sit like this for the rest of my life," Dorothy argued.

Beatrice smiled and nuzzled her face into Dorothy's hair. In a while, they would get up and she would rearrange her clothes, and they could retire to private quarters to have a proper reunion. But for now she was content to recline against Dorothy and watch the window.

The sun was going to set soon, and she couldn't think of a better way to watch it.

EPILOGUE

A WEEK after their return, Dorothy dressed in her finest suit and walked to the Inkwell for her reckoning. She and Beatrice had barely left the townhouse since their return to London. They both still needed to do some healing after their ordeals. While they slept, got reacquainted with each other, and tended to the damage that had been done to the house, Trafalgar and the rest of the Mnemosyne Society could deliberate and eventually come to a decision on how to proceed with Dorothy's membership.

When they'd first arrived home, Dorothy had taken Trafalgar aside and brought up the inevitable trial. "Tell the rest of the Society that no matter what they decide, it won't affect my contributions. The books in the library, my vault, everything that the others have utilized over the years will still be accessible to them regardless of my status."

"That's very generous of you," Trafalgar said.

Dorothy shrugged. "I want them to choose *me*. Not my stuff."

Trafalgar nodded. "I'll let them know."

Ordinarily she would have spent the intervening time dreading their verdict, but she quickly discovered she didn't care. She had Beatrice. She felt at peace with whatever they decided. She would be happy to spend the rest of her days in her home, with her lover, drawing maps. It would be enough for her as long as they were together.

When she was finally summoned, she walked to the tavern with no dread or anticipation. She trusted the people in charge of the decision, people who had been her friends at one point, and she was well aware of how she had treated them the past few years. She was confident whatever choice they made would be fair and just.

The Council were the only members present when she arrived. Leonard and Agnes Keeping were well enough to make the trip, and Dorothy went over to their table and greeted them warmly. It had been years since she'd seen them, for which she apologized profusely and was just as thoroughly forgiven. Cecil Dubourne had also made the trip from America. She didn't know if that was a good omen for her chances or a nail in her coffin. Trafalgar and Violet were sat at the bar, with Cora standing near them.

Dorothy stood in the center of the room and looked around. "Is Ivy here somewhere?"

"No," Trafalgar said. "No one has heard from her since that night at Threadneedle when she attempted to break you out."

"I'm sure she'll make her presence known before long," Dorothy said, although this time she wasn't sure. She looked around at the gathered faces before she settled on Cora. "I assume my summons means you've come to an agreement."

"We have. Is Beatrice coming...?"

"No," Dorothy said. "She decided to voluntarily withdraw from the Society. She'll offer her services when necessary but she doesn't feel like she would be very useful without her powers. I think she also wants some time to adjust to her... new circumstances."

"That's understandable," Cora said.

Dorothy nodded and finally looked at Trafalgar. "As for me...?"

Trafalgar realized she had been tacitly elected as spokesperson. She looked at Violet and cleared her throat.

"We appreciate that you were suffering from tremendous grief over the past few years. But that doesn't excuse your actions. You were reckless, you threatened the lives and safety of every member of this group, and you withheld information. These infractions cannot be ignored. But we must also take your vast contributions to the Society into account. We would not have formed without you. Most of us would not be alive without you.

"So we have decided that you will remain a member in good standing, but you are no longer a voting member of the Council. In fact, you wield no power whatsoever in the decision-making process.

You will be the lowest-ranking member of the Society, below every apprentice, for a probationary period of one year. After that time, you will be allowed to advance in the ranks. By that time, several apprentices will have achieved seniority. They will be considered for Council positions before you are."

Cora said, "Are these terms acceptable to you?"

Dorothy sighed and shrugged. "Considering what I've done to you, I believe this is kinder than I deserve. Thank you for your leniency."

Agnes Keeping said, "The Society hasn't been the same without you, Dorothy."

Leonard added, "And a lack of seniority or voting power doesn't mean you're silenced. We'll still listen to your opinions. Take them into advisement."

"I appreciate that."

Violet clapped her hands. "All right. Now that all the sordid business of punishment is out of the way..." She swept behind the bar and pulled down two bottles and held them aloft. "Let's get down to the true business of this get-together and drink!"

"A splendid idea!" Trafalgar said, slapping the bar.

Dorothy accepted a glass and spent a fair amount of time catching up with Cora, enough time to be polite, and then excused herself to go out into the courtyard. She dusted the fallen leaves from a concrete bench and sat down, her head tilted back to watch the clouds.

She had only been outside a few minutes when Trafalgar found her. She hesitated in the doorway and nodded at the bench.

"May I sit? I understand if you'd rather be alone."

"No, please."

Trafalgar came out and sat down. She left enough space between them for another person. Together they watched the clouds, sipped their wine, and randomly shuffled their shoes on the patio. Dorothy traced lines with the toe of her boot.

"Is Trix well?"

"She's doing very well, yes," Dorothy said, grateful for an easy topic of conversation. "She has some issues with insomnia. She'll sleep at strange hours during the day, then she'll be awake all night. But we're trying to find a comfortable balance for her. We're making progress. The strangest thing is food. Her tastes have changed. And we're struggling to determine her age. She never knew when she was actually born, so it had always been guesswork. But now we have to decide whether to add in or skip the seven years she was incorporeal."

Trafalgar nodded. "It's an interesting question. And one without precedent."

"Mm-hmm." Dorothy looked into her wine. "I've heard what the Society decided. I'd like to know how you voted, if that's all right."

Trafalgar sighed. "I think it will be easier to calculate Beatrice's age than explain how I feel about your continued presence in the Society. To be blunt, I don't know. I had no qualms working with you in Turkey, but I can't say whether or not I'd be willing to repeat the experience. But we're both members of the Society so I'm sure it will happen eventually. But as for us, the partnership... no, Dorothy. My feelings on that haven't changed. That's over. Trafalgar and Boone have had their final adventure."

"A pity," Dorothy said. "But you seem to have found an amazing new partner. Rhys Tracking and Investigative Services."

Trafalgar smiled. "She is a worthy companion in every sense of the word, yes. And I owe you for opening my eyes to possibilities I wouldn't have considered otherwise. If I'd never known you, I would have considered Violet a very dear friend and nothing more."

"I'm proud to have helped you find your person."

"Mm." Trafalgar chuckled and nodded. "Yes. And you are obviously aware that your position with the Society is..." She waved her hand vaguely in front of her. "It doesn't have to dictate your actual work. You've always been independent. You can do the same thing you always did before the group was created."

"True. But it's hard to feel any purpose now that Beatrice is back. I've spent so much time dedicated to that singular goal."

"There's a whole world out there," Trafalgar said. "And you certainly have the time. You did something that no one else has ever survived. You did it four times, and you were recovered within a few days. That's enough proof for me to believe you're immortal."

"At least I *was* immortal. The water pulled four lifetimes out of me. Who knows how much is actually left? Maybe it all balanced out and I'll have a relatively normal lifetime."

"That's still a very long time, potentially. Magic may have been greatly diminished, but there are still people out there with powers they don't control and don't understand. They'll need help from experts, and we're about as close as the world will get. And the artifact you discovered! My word, Dorothy, you uncovered an easy method of traveling in time. Even if there are moral issues about how it should be utilized, it's still a powerful tool."

"Powerful and inaccurate. But you are correct. There are more mysteries to be solved. More people to helped." She finished off her wine and bent down to put the glass down on the ground between her feet. She sat up with a sigh and leaned back to look up at the clouds. "I was so wrong, Trafalgar. And so convinced I was right that I could have destroyed the entire world. I can't understate how grateful I am to you for bringing me back to my senses."

"Always. No matter what else is happening, I'll always be there to knock you down a peg when you need it."

Dorothy laughed. Trafalgar finished her glass and put it down on the bench between them.

The knot of anxiety that had been gathered at the nape of Dorothy's neck relaxed itself. They sat together, the silence less uncomfortable than it had been when Trafalgar first came out, and Dorothy allowed herself to enjoy it. Nothing had ended, only changed. They weren't partners and would likely never again consider themselves such, but they were still friends. Or, if they weren't quite there yet, the possibility existed for them to get there one day. There were countless mysteries to solve, hidden treasures to uncover, forgotten people who needed to be brought to the light.

The road forward was unfamiliar, but she was confident they would be able to navigate it well. And if not, they could always lean on each other when the going became too hazardous.

She bent down and picked up her empty glass, holding it toward Trafalgar. "It was a pleasure being your partner. To the intrepid Trafalgar Rhys."

Trafalgar smiled and picked up her own glass. "To the immortal Lady Boone. Be it figurative or literal, your name will live on far into the future."

They tapped glasses and smiled at each other.

The world was a wild, wonderful, weird place. She couldn't wait to see what it had in store for them.

ABOUT THE AUTHOR

Geonn Cannon is the author of over fifty novels, including the Riley Parra series which was adapted into an Emmy-nominated webseries by Tello Films. He's also written two tie-in novels for the television series Stargate SG-1. He was the first male author to win a Golden Crown Literary Society Award for his novel *Gemini*, and he won a second for *Dogs of War*. Information about his other works and an archive of free stories can be found online at geonncannon.com.

Prize Fighter

Six years ago, professional boxer Max "Wrecker" Reszke lost control in the ring. One moment of blind rage put her opponent into a coma from which she never woke. Though cleared of any criminal charges, Max hangs up her gloves and swears that she'll never risk losing control like that again.

Until one night, a chance encounter in an alley, a damsel in distress. Max leaps into action and saves the stranger. She soon learns that the woman she saved is actress Renee Lamar. Renee, anxious and paranoid about security, offers to reward Max's chivalry with a job as her bodyguard.

Max has nothing to lose by agreeing, but soon discovers Renee might be her own worst enemy. Half a decade after leaving the ring, Max faces a new fight that can't be won with fists.

Into the Furnace

Kelly Lake comes from a family of firefighters, but she still had to prove herself to her brothers and her father before they accepted her as one of their own. On her days off she tends bar at the firehouse hangout across the street and spends time trying to breathe life into a relationship she knows is doomed. Her life is cruising along just fine until the day her squad responds to a horrific arson that will cause her carefully-orchestrated balancing act to come falling down around her. The blaze claims the lives of eleven people, half of them children, and the fire department takes the blame.

Kelly soon finds herself at the center of a media firestorm when she inadvertently becomes the poster girl for the incident. The trauma of the fire is compounded by her personal house of cards collapsing. Her relationship begins showing its cracks at the same time long-buried family secrets rear their ugly heads. Attacked from all angles, Kelly starts thinking the only place she'll be safe is running headlong into the furnace.

"Easily one of the best samplings of queer fiction I've had the pleasure to read in a very long time. I could not recommend it more, and sincerely hope that upon its release in November Into the Furnace will light the same fire in each of your hearts that it has already lit in mine." - Tabitha Beth, The Rainbow Hub.